TWISTED FLAMES

Borgo Press Books by Victor J. Banis

TWISTED FLAMES

VICTOR J. BANIS

Writing as Victor Jay

THE BORGO PRESS

MMXII

TWISTED FLAMES

FIRST BORGO PRESS EDITION

Published by Wildside Press LLC

www.wildsidebooks.com

TWISTED FLAMES

CONTENTS

CHAPTER ONE

From the window of her hotel room, Laura Anderson looked down at the streets of Los Angeles below. The city buzzed with the early evening activity, and endless stream of cars dashing past, crowds of people everywhere, the lights making evening into day. Streams of cars poured swiftly by.

Despite the two weeks since she had first arrived here, the city was still strange to her. Everything was so different from Indiana, from Terre Haute. She couldn't even say if she liked it. She thought not, nor that she ever would—but she told herself with a sigh that she might as well get used to it. This was going to be her home, probably for the rest of her life.

She turned from the window, turning her back on the city outside. She could be grateful at least that she wouldn't be living here, in the heart of the city, with all its confusion and endless activity. She would be at Sandy Knoll—even the name had a serene quality that was different from downtown Los Angeles. Of course, it was a tract development, but only a small one. She closed her eyes and imagined the house in which she would soon be living.

Yes, of course, it looked very much like the other houses in the tract, but she intended to make hers different. She would plant flowers and shrubs, something suited to the sandy soil—the house was near the beach. And she was happy for that, too, the long expanse of white sand that lay just beyond the patio of her new home. And there was the mighty ocean itself, beyond the beach, and so unlike anything she had known in Indiana.

Yes, she felt sure she would be happy in her new house, with its ocean setting. She would be happy with her new husband, too. But she had no sooner thought that than she felt a sense of uneasiness. She glanced at the clock on the dresser. Neil Abbot would be arriving here any minute. He'd promised her a night on the town—cocktails and dinner in a special restaurant, and afterward even a visit to the legendary nightclub, The Coconut Grove. Their last night as sweethearts. Tomorrow they would be man and wife, newlyweds. Mr. and Mrs. Neil Abbott, in their new house in Sandy Knoll. She felt another twinge of uneasiness, but did not linger on it.

"Well, tonight you're still Laura Anderson," she told her reflection in the mirror. "And your husband to be will be here any minute, expecting you to be dressed and ready."

Laura Abbot. She'd even commented to Neil how convenient it was that she needn't even change her initials. The letter A on the towels she had bought long before for her hope-chest could just as well stand for

Abbot as Anderson.

She quickly undressed and showered, careful not to get her hair wet—she had splurged earlier and had it done at an expensive shop just down the street—an extravagance, to be sure, but she wanted to look her best for Neil. And without conceit she knew that her best was pretty good. She had been Miss Indiana only a couple of years earlier, and before that Miss Harvest Festival.

She paused coming out of the shower and looked at herself in the full length mirror on the bathroom door. Her auburn hair fell in soft waves about her oval face. Her features were regular, her eyes vivid green and set wide. She supposed her mouth was a bit too full, but men had never seemed to mind that—nor with the lovely body the mirror showed back to her—soft of shoulder, pale, her skin as smooth and pink as a baby's. Her full round breasts were altogether womanly, however, full and round, needing no support, the wide aureoles thrusting brazenly forward. Wide curvaceous hips flared from her thin waist and the curve of her belly led downward to the darkness between her creamy thighs. Yes, she knew that men found her desirable.

The phone rang. She wrapped herself in a bath towel and went to answer it as she emerged from the steamy bathroom. She wrapped the towel loosely around her body and went to answer the summons. Neil Abbott's voice greeted her from the other end.

"Oh, you're early!" she cried when she recognized

Neil's voice on the phone.

"Umm, I think it's you that's late," he said. "Aren't you ready?"

"It won't take me long to dress," she assured him, aware that he was somewhat annoyed by her habitual tardiness. "Why don't you come on up here and wait?"

There was a slight pause before Neil answered. "I could wait in the bar just as easily. It might look better if I did."

"Don't be silly," she insisted. "After all, we're practically married, you know. And besides, this is the wicked city of Los Angeles. No one will bat an eyelash over it."

He laughed at that, although the voice sounded to her a little strained. "I guess you're right. I'll be up in a minute or two."

Laura returned the receiver to its cradle and stood thoughtfully in the center of the room, thinking of Neil Abbot, the man she would marry in a few hours. Why was it that after all this time she suddenly felt so unsure? It had been bothering her since she arrived in the city two weeks ago.

It wasn't as though she didn't know him. They were from the same city, and Terre Haute wasn't so big a city. Neil, four years older than she, had been in college when she was in high school. But even then she had loved him, as had almost every other girl who was in school with her. What girl wouldn't have loved Neil, the big football star, the local hero?

When he had asked her to marry him, right after

his graduation from college, there had not been the slightest doubt in her mind. She had accepted at once. There was a job waiting for Neil in California, and it had been decided that he would come west, get started on the job and find them a house. Then, when everything was nicely in order, he would come back for her.

Everything had gone well and according to the schedule, at first. Neil's letters kept her well informed of his progress in the new job, and she heard at once when he found the house, which he described as "just what we want". The date was set for the wedding and the preparations made. Then there had been the accident.

For two months Neil remained in the hospital. The wedding was postponed indefinitely. Finally, Neil had been released. Things still had to be delayed, however. He had been gone from his work for so long, it was difficult to take more time off. Weeks had passed and Laura's impatience had grown until she had at last reached a decision on her own. If Neil could not come to Terre Haute to marry her, she would go to California. At first, Neil had resisted the suggestion but in time he had relented. So here she was.

Like any young bride, she had looked forward to a more elaborate affair than the simple civil ceremony on the morrow, but she knew that it was just as well this way. Her parents had not really been in a position to afford the wedding as it had been planned. They had mortgaged their modest home. Because of the change in plans, they had been able to repay the loan and spare themselves the financial burden. This way, everything was quick and uncomplicated.

Except, she reminded herself, for this nagging doubt. Throughout the year of waiting, she had remained firmly convinced that she and Neil were truly meant for one another, that their love was beyond question. But since arriving in Los Angeles, she had become less certain with each passing day. It had begun the very first day, when she came down the ramp from the airplane and saw Neil waiting for her. It suddenly occurred to her then that he was almost a stranger to her.

She had seen Neil every evening since arriving in the city. Their time together was pleasant. Arrangements for the wedding had been made prompt and efficient. She had seen the new house, approved his selection, and the two of them had spent considerable time shopping for furnishings.

Yet now, on the very eve of her marriage, Laura was unable to shake the gloomy feeling that she was making a mistake. She had tried to view her emotions honestly, still she did not know whether her feeling for Neil was love or mere schoolgirl infatuation with the most popular boy in Terre Haute.

The knock at the door interrupted her train of thought. Neil was already there and she had not even begun to dress. She wrapped the towel more carefully about herself and hurried to answer the door.

It would be difficult for any girl not to have a crush on him, she thought, as she opened the door and saw

Neil Abbot standing there. Dark and ruggedly hand-some, Neil stood six feet, two inches tall and although he was slimmer now than he had been in his football playing days, he looked nonetheless every inch a man, big and powerful. Grinning at her as he was now, she was almost able to resolve all of the doubts that she had in her mind—almost, but not quite.

"When you said you had to dress, you weren't kidding were you?" he quipped. He came inside, closing the door after himself, and reached for her.

Laura came into his arms easily, gladly. It was only when she was close to him like this that she felt sure of herself and of their marriage. At other times they seemed to be making believe. She had wondered more than once if he were not having exactly the same doubts that she was suffering. But there was no hesitation in his kiss. His mouth sought hers with undeniable ardor. Her lips opened to him and her tongue darted play-fully. She could smell the clean, male scent of him, feel the powerful muscles of his arms pinning her close to him.

"Oh, Neil!" she whispered, burying her face in the curve of one brawny shoulder. He kissed her again, tilting her face upward, crushing her to him. Her breasts were pressed tightly against his chest. His hand, of its own accord, slid eagerly downward to the flaring buttocks beneath the towel that provided a scant covering for her body.

Laura felt herself begin to throb with excitement. She remembered again their last date in Terre Haute, a date that had ended in an orgy of passion which initiated her into the wonders and joy of love. Neil had been the first for her and the fire he had kindled still burned brightly within her.

The memory of that ecstatic night often tortured her until she thought she could not endure another moment without the sort of bliss that Neil had given her. Yet, strangely, since she had arrived in Los Angeles, there had been no such incident, nothing more than fervent kisses that awakened her and left her utterly frustrated. She told herself he was being honorable toward her, playing the role of the gentleman. But now she wanted him to know that the desire was as much hers as his. After all, they would be married before another twenty four hours passed. It couldn't matter much what they did now. And perhaps his uninhibited love would resolve her doubts.

With one hand she tugged at the corner of the towel where she had tied it about her body. It came loose, and the towel fell away from her. She was naked and trembling in his arms, ready for his love.

"Laura!" he gasped excitedly, his hands grasping at the naked flesh revealed to him.

She stepped backward leading him along and found the bed, lowering herself to its smooth, clean surface. He came down upon it with her, his eyes wide with passion as they swept over her loveliness. His huge hands went for her breasts, fondling them eagerly. She felt his lips upon one rigid, trembling nipple. His hands sought her hot, fragrant thighs. Boldly, eagerly, Laura reached for him, wanting to savor his body as he was savoring hers, eager to possess him.

He cringed at her touch, and sat up suddenly, pulling away from her in one quick, violent movement.

"Neil, what's wrong?" she asked, startled by the sudden change of mood. Why on earth should he have pulled away from her as he did? Now he was actually standing, turning his back on her nakedness.

"I can't marry you," he told her, his voice little more than a whisper.

"What do you mean, you can't?" she wanted to know. She stood also, reaching for him. Again he moved away from her.

"I just can't that's all!" He was suddenly angry. She couldn't understand the reason for it. A moment ago he had been about to make ardent love to her, and now he was furious about something that she could not comprehend.

Laura took a deep breath trying to calm herself. Her body tingled with unfulfilled desire, but she knew that would have to wait until she had helped him with whatever was bothering him.

"Is there someone else?" she asked, her voice deliberately even and unemotional.

He turned back toward her, and she saw tears in his eyes. He was not angry after all, but hurt about something.

"Neil, what is it? You must tell me, please!"

She went to him again, throwing her arms protectively about him. This time he did not move away, nor did he return her embrace.

"I haven't told you everything," he said finally. She said nothing, but waited anxiously for him to continue.

"About the accident," he went on, speaking slowly. "The car and I were both pretty torn up, you know."

"Yes, but you're all right now," she argued with him. "You said there would be some scars on your back, but that doesn't matter to me. And you're fine other than that...."

"I wish I were," he snapped abruptly. He looked away again, and held her gently from him. "Laura, I was wounded...a piece of glass cut me...." He stopped, all but choking on the words.

Suddenly she knew what he was trying to explain to her.

"Neil, you're not trying to tell me...." She could not bring herself to say it either.

"...That I'll never be a husband to you." He said it coldly, as though he wanted to hurt her as he had been hurt.

Laura's arms dropped limply to her sides. She moved slowly away, across to the window, and stared down again at the street scene below.

"Never?" she managed to ask after a few minutes.

Behind her, Neil sighed wearily. "I don't know. Maybe in time something can be done. But for now it's hopeless. I've tried. Before you got here, I tried with several girls. I even tried again last night, after I brought you back here. I hoped there'd be a change. There wasn't!"

Laura stood for another moment in silence. A short while ago she had wondered whether she should marry this man. Now she knew she would have to do so, and she knew also that it would mean unhappiness for her.

"It doesn't matter," she said aloud, forcing a smile to her lips. "We can be married anyway, just as we've planned. Everything will work out all right, you'll see."

"I can't let you marry me out of pity." He sat down on the edge of the bed as he said it.

He was right, she knew. She *was* marrying him out of pity. But what else could she do? Certainly it would have been unspeakably cruel of her to turn him down, and surely he had already suffered enough. Later, when he became more accustomed to the fact, adjusted to it, perhaps they could do something—have the marriage annulled, perhaps. Or maybe his condition would improve. But she could not bring herself to add to his unhappiness—even if it meant sacrificing her own happiness.

"It isn't pity," she said. "I love you, and that hasn't changed in the least. We'll go right ahead and get married tomorrow, and everything will work out all right."

He looked up and studied her, so long and searchingly that she felt certain he must know what she was thinking. He smiled a strange, almost cynical, smile.

"If I were any kind of a man," he said, one hand tracing its way over the softness of her naked hips, "I wouldn't let you do this. But I'm not strong enough to do what I know is right. I want you, Laura. If you'll still have me, we'll get married tomorrow."

"Of course, I'll have you," she assured him.

She closed her eyes as he enfolded her in his strong embrace once more. She had committed herself now. Somehow they would work things out.

But how, she wondered, was she going to contend with the desire coursing through her vibrant young body. She had counted on Neil Abbot, her husband, to answer the needs of her ardent body. Were they to go unsatisfied—and for how long?

CHAPTER TWO

Laura woke early in the morning, after a night of uneasy sleep and confused dreams. For hours after Neil had brought her back to the hotel, she had tossed and turned on her bed, thinking about the awkward position in which she found herself.

To marry Neil now, knowing what she did about his condition, might prove a terrible mistake for both of them. If she were more certain of her love for him, if she could depend upon that love for the strength needed, things might work out. Other women had faced such problems and presumably found a way of living with them. But without the overwhelming love that had guided those others, could she hope to find a way?

Even as she considered those questions, however, she knew that she hadn't the heart to break off the engagement. Whether her love for Neil was profound or not, she did feel an affection for him, and certainly sympathy. She could not bring herself to add to his misery. The breaking of any engagement at such a late date, practically at the altar, could be a hard blow to the ego.

Ultimately, there was only one decision she could rightfully make. She must sacrifice her own immediate happiness, set aside the doubts and fears in her mind, do what she thought best for Neil. In time, perhaps....

With a weary sigh, she rose from the bed, feeling tired and quite unlike a woman who, in a few hours, was to be married.

Neil arrived later in the morning. She knew, from his expression and the unaccustomed shyness of his manner, that he too was less than certain of their course of action. The knowledge only renewed her determination to mask her own uncertainties. She met his hesitant greeting with a warm smile and an assumed confidence.

"You see, for once, I'm ready," she declared, pirouetting so that he could admire her appearance. She had purchased her outfit in Los Angeles, remembering with longing the beautiful gown of satin and lace that had initially been selected for their church wedding. Instead, she wore a white street dress, simple and unextravagant, and a wisp of a hat that left her auburn hair unhidden.

"You're still sure?" Neil asked. Although her eager manner had erased some of the tension from his face, he was still far from confident. "There's still time to back out if you want to."

For an instant she almost surrendered to her own fear. Then she checked herself, still smiling.

"Of course I'm sure. What time are we supposed to be there?"

"Eleven." He seemed to accept her decision as final, although he showed no special enthusiasm. "We've got time for some breakfast."

"I don't think I could eat anything, but I'll have some coffee while you eat."

Neil lifted one eyebrow. "Scared?" he asked, lighting a cigarette for her.

"Not scared—excited!" she insisted, accepting the cigarette gratefully. Her stomach was truly tingling with butterflies. "It isn't every day a girl gets married, you know."

He returned her smile as they left the hotel. Neil decided that he was not hungry either, so they found a nearby coffee shop and drank several cups of strong black brew while they waited for the time to pass.

Laura's nervousness continued to increase with each passing moment. *There's still time,* she told herself. She could still back out, before the damage was done. Stubbornly, she resisted the urge, forcing a show of eager confidence.

It was time at last. Neil did not ask her again if she were still certain, although he gave her a long, questioning look as they approached the parking lot and the waiting car....

* * * * * * *

"Well, Mrs. Abbott, that's that." Neil held her arm as he led her once again to his car. "How does it feel to be married?"

"Do you know, I don't feel a bit different," Laura

answered.

Actually, she did feel different. At the conclusion of the simple ceremony, she felt as though a door had slammed shut behind her. She had committed herself to a course of action that increasingly terrified her. They were now officially man and wife, but there was none of the giddy delirium that should have accompanied that fact. She was sure that Neil was as glum and dispirited as she although he, too, was making an effort at cheerfulness. Other couples had so much to look forward to on this occasion, not the least of which was the complete bliss that the wedding night promised—the pleasure denied to her and Neil.

Neil drove back to her hotel. They had lunch there, neither of them doing more than picking over their food. Laura's bags were already packed, so it took mere minutes to check out of the hotel. Then they were on their way to Sandy Knoll and their new home.

Laura watched with interest as the passing scene became more obviously beach-oriented. The highway carried them north, following the shoreline and she began to recognize landmarks that indicated Sandy Knoll was near.

"I'll devote myself to making a home for us," she promised herself silently. "In that way, I'll compensate for everything that our marriage lacks."

Even as she made the promise, however, doubts began to nag at her again. There might be some things that could not be compensated.

They arrived shortly. A drive led off of the highway,

through a rather pompous-looking arch that seemed out of place, and brought them to Sandy Knoll. Despite the similarity of the houses, a complaint common to most tract developments, it was not difficult to identify their house. Actually, only five or six of the houses were complete. They were, in a sense, pioneers, and had jokingly referred to themselves as such while furnishing the house.

All but one of the completed dwellings stood clustered close to the beach on one of the several unfinished streets. Their house was the last one, a simple, unadorned unit painted a light-hearted yellow and white.

Laura tried to envision, as they drove up to the garage, how she would finish the lawn. She made a mental note to begin by learning what would grow in the sandy soil. The climate, she reminded herself, was far different from that of Indiana. Lilacs would be impossible, regardless of the fact that they were her favorite flower. No doubt some of the neighbor women would be able to offer suggestions.

"You're home, Mrs. Abbott," Neil announced, switching off the ignition.

"So I see, Mr. Abbott," Laura answered. She clambered out of the car without waiting for him to come around and open the door for her. The air was cooler than in the city, and carried with it the unmistakable scent of the ocean.

She started toward the front door, but Neil caught up with her and held her arm firmly.

"You don't think I'd let you *walk* across the threshold," he said. He darted ahead of her, unlocked the front door and came lightly back down the steps. Laura was laughing with genuine pleasure when he swept her up in his strong arms and carried her easily up the steps and into the house.

CHAPTER THREE

They laughed gaily as they entered the house, both of them for a fleeting moment carefree and happy.

"Enter the typical newlyweds," Laura declared, hugging Neil's neck.

Neil's smile faded and became a frown.

"Well, almost," he said glumly, lowering her to her feet with almost rude abruptness.

They stood in silence for a moment, looking about the room. They had been there often in the two weeks past, preparing the house and arranging the new furniture. It was comfortable in good taste. The decor was mostly Danish Modern, inexpensive but good pieces. Laura had made many plans for further decorations of the house. Now those plans seemed pointless to her.

"How about a drink?" Neil suggested in a quick attempt to restore their spirits.

Laura scowled. "It's early in the day for that, isn't it?"

"It's our wedding day, remember?" He led her firmly toward the small bar built into one end of the living room. "People have a right to break the rules on their wedding day."

A new doubt crept into Laura's mind as she remembered the two weeks just past. Neil drank rather frequently, although she could not remember him drinking at all before. She had paid little attention to this fact, dismissing it as caused by the nervousness natural in a bridegroom. Now, however, she could understand that other factors had played a part, and she wondered how much he had come to rely upon alcohol as a solution to his problems. It was another area in which she realized she knew little about her husband.

"I guess you have a point there," she relented, wanting to avoid dissension at the moment. Surely he would relax more now that they were actually married, and his drinking would be unnecessary. She went along with him, seating herself on one of the tall stools. Neil went behind the bar and produced a bottle of Bourbon.

"We have Bourbon and Bourbon," he quipped. "What'll it be?"

"That's a tough question. How about Bourbon?"

He brought two glasses from the shelf underneath the bar. "Ice!" he demanded imperiously.

"Ice," she repeated and jumped down to hurry to the kitchen. She was back a moment later with a tray of ice and a pitcher of water. Neil poured the drinks, leaving little room, she noticed, for water.

"Here's to us." He toasted her, handing her one of the glasses.

Laura returned the toast and sipped the drink cautiously. It burned slightly as it went down. She was not much accustomed to drinking, and moreover she had eaten little lunch.

The lack of lunch, however, did not seem to worry Neil. He downed his drink rapidly and poured himself a second before she had done more than taste hers.

"Hey, you *are* celebrating, aren't you?" She tried to make her tone light and joking, but in fact she was frightened by his intensity. It was as though he were determined to get as drunk as possible, as quickly as possible.

In answer, he tilted his glass up again. Laura held her tongue, reminding herself that he had every reason to be nervous. If liquor would help to restore his spirits, there was probably no harm in it, and it certainly seemed to be doing just that. He was smiling pleasantly, his eyes gleaming perhaps a little too brightly.

"It's a rotten shame we can't take a honeymoon," he said, wiping his mouth with the back of his hand.

Laura shrugged and allowed herself to relax a little. The drink helped her nerves also.

"We'll make up for it," she told him with a smile.

"You're damned right we will," he agreed loudly. "I promise you a first-class honeymoon next year. Where would you like to go—Paris? Rome? Say the word and your husband will take you there."

The word husband brought Laura's tension back with a flurry. Her *husband!* Looking at him, clearly feeling the effects of his liquor, she realized once again that they were strangers to one another in a very real sense. Worse, they were without the all-important link that gave most couples the opportunity to comprehend and join with one another.

She was spared the necessity of an answer by the doorbell.

"We've got company," she said aloud. "Our first visitors in our new home."

"It's the back door," Neil told her as she started toward the front.

With a grin, Laura went in that direction, across the compact kitchen, to the door that opened to the patio in the rear.

Her first impression of the woman standing outside the door was one of breathtaking loveliness. The stranger was taller than she, slightly more slender. Her age, Laura guessed, was somewhere between twenty and thirty-five. Gleaming black hair, cut stylishly short, framed a narrow face that was dominated by hauntingly dark eyes. The brightly patterned blouse and skin-tight capri pants she wore set off her trim, youthful figure to the best possible advantage.

"Hello." Laura greeted her visitor meekly. She felt almost unattractive in the presence of this sleek, striking creature.

"Hello. I'm Eve Blair." Her visitor returned the greeting with a flash of white teeth. "One of your neighbors. I saw you arrive and thought I'd better come over and welcome you to the underworld."

A strange way to describe the neighborhood, Laura thought, but she found the gesture flattering. It was comforting to know that she was among friendly people.

"Come in," she said, opening the door wide. "We're just having a drink." Then, thinking that this might create an unfavorable impression, she added quickly "We're newlyweds."

"I noticed." Eve Blair's smile was not particularly pleasant, as though she were mocking everything that she saw or heard. Laura blushed, remembering how Neil had carried her across the threshold, announcing the newness of their marriage to any onlookers.

That's silly, she told herself, leading the way into the living room. *There's no reason to be ashamed of my marriage or embarrassed by it.* But somehow, aware of Eve's dark eyes on her as they walked, she had the impression that this beautiful woman could see through the sham they were putting up, could somehow know the truth about the marriage.

Neil had already started on another drink when they entered the room. Laura saw his eyes take in their guest and glimmer even more brightly with appreciation. For an instant, she suffered a pang of jealousy. *That's ridiculous,* she told herself, almost laughing aloud. *That's one thing I won't have to worry about.* Physically, at least, there was no likelihood that Neil would be unfaithful to her.

"Neil, this is Eve Blair. She's one of our neighbors, and she came by to wish us welcome."

"Now that's what I call hospitality," Neil said loudly. "I hope you'll have a drink with us.

"And that's what I call hospitality," Eve answered him, settling herself gracefully on the other stool.

"You've talked me into it."

Laura watched with bitter amusement as Eve's eyes took in Neil's large, husky body, her admiration unconcealed. *If only she knew,* Laura thought to herself. What would Eve Blair have done, faced with the same decision? Would she have sacrificed her own physical needs for the sake of a man who was incapable of performing sexually. Studying the dark beauty, Laura found the prospect unlikely.

Eve accepted her drink with a warm smile at Neil, and turned toward Laura. "I don't suppose you'd consider loaning him out," she said with a nod in Neil's direction.

"I don't think so," Laura answered, trying to keep her tone light and bantering.

"That's just what she says," Neil commented.

Laura blushed at the exchange. Surely Neil wouldn't create embarrassment for them both by revealing the truth about their marriage.

"Will I sound smug if I say I've got nothing to worry about?" Laura asked aloud, with a cold glance in Neil's direction.

He laughed again, but said nothing more. Eve Blair looked from one to the other of them, apparently weighing the situation. What conclusions she reached Laura could not guess, but of one thing she was certain: Eve had not been entirely joking when she made the suggestion. Everything about the woman was sensual, hinting at wanton desire for physical sensation.

"Well, I imagine the two of you will keep one another

quite well entertained for a while," she said dryly.

They sat for a moment in silence. Laura felt uncomfortable in the other woman's presence, and was painfully aware that Neil was rapidly drinking himself into a stupor.

"May I say, your husband is a very fortunate man?" Eve said finally, breaking the silence.

Laura turned in Eve's direction, flattered by the compliment, but the words of thanks caught in her throat as her eyes met the other, darker pair.

The impression was gone at once, but the shock stayed with Laura, lingering in her awareness. Had she been mistaken, or had she seen in Eve's eyes the same frank admiration, even desire, that had been directed a moment before toward Neil?

Surely not, she assured herself. True, she had heard of such things. She knew, mostly from books she had read, that some women did have an attraction for other women. But certainly there was no reason to suspect Eve Blair of that sort of perversion. After all, the woman was married—or presumably so. Eve had not specifically made any comments on her own marital status.

"What sort of work does your husband do?" Laura asked aloud, wanting to reassure herself on that point.

"Hank?" Eve said the name with a shrug that made Hank Blair seem like the most unimportant subject in the world. "Oh, he sells insurance. At least that's what it says on his income-tax return. Most of his time is spent hopping from one bed to another."

Laura blushed at the boldness of the statement. Eve Blair might be married, but it was evident that the marriage was not a very romantic one.

"What about you, Neil," Eve was saying, directing her attention once more in his direction. "With that build, you must be an athlete."

Neil swelled with noticeable pride although, in his drunken condition, he did not look particularly athletic to Laura.

"I was," he answered proudly. "In school. Now I'm an aeronautical engineer. At least that's what it says on my income-tax return."

Eve laughed aloud at that. "Touché," she answered, lifting her glass in a salute before she drained it. "It sounds terribly intellectual."

"Not really. I'm a stress analyst, actually. I look for the weak spots in planes, and make recommendations for the design."

Laura remembered the past. How enthusiastic Neil had been about his job when he got it, and how often and long he had talked about it! It occurred to her that he had scarcely mentioned it at all since she had arrived in Los Angeles.

Eve stood, stretching her shoulders lazily.

"I won't make a pest of myself, not just yet. Incidentally, if you should be bored with one another's company, we're having a little get-together for the neighbors tonight. Nothing fancy, just the typical all-American barbecue. Feel welcome to join us."

"Thank you," Laura said, standing also. "We won't

be bored with one another, but we'd love to come. It would give us a chance to meet our neighbors."

"Don't thank me until you've met them," Eve told her, starting toward the back door. "You may regret the decision. I'm in the house next door—but you'll see us gathered joyously about the patio. Come whenever you feel up to it."

Laura moved impulsively to show her out, but Eve waved away the gesture with a brisk sweep of her hand.

"I know the way. This house is exactly like mine, you know."

With that, she was gone. Laura found herself staring after the woman. Her initial reaction to Eve's visit had been one of gratitude and pleasure. She had been happy to learn that her neighbors were the friendly, sociable sort.

Now, with the visit concluded, her feelings were mixed. Eve Blair impressed her as altogether too friendly, and not in a mere neighborly way. Laura wondered about the others. The evening, she concluded, should be interesting, if nothing else.

CHAPTER FOUR

Laura's uneasiness increased as the day wore on. Neil continued to drink steadily, although not as heavily as at first. She hesitated to say anything to him, lest their first day of marriage be spoiled by a quarrel. For a time she considered postponing the introductions to their neighbors, not wishing to appear with a drunken husband. But as evening approached, Neil seemed to be safely in control of himself, so she decided that all would go well after all.

She saw Eve Blair come out to her patio late in the afternoon. A short time later she was joined by a man who Laura took to be her husband.

Looking at Hank Blair, Laura wondered what reason Eve could have for interest in other men. Even from her distant kitchen, he gave every impression of being man enough for any woman. He was physically a brute of a man, taller even than Neil and huskier. Dark curly hair gave him almost a shaggy appearance, although his dress and grooming were, in general, neat. It was easy to see that he was attractive to women.

Still, if he were as unfaithful as his wife had implied, then Eve had justification for her cynicisms.

The pair were joined shortly by a lone woman and another couple, and Laura decided it was time that she and Neil made their appearance. Neil had showered and shaved, and there was no obvious reason for anyone to suspect that he had been drinking. If he was feeling any ill effects, they were well concealed.

Eve Blair spotted them as they came out the back door and waved a greeting. The two patios were separated only by a patch of green grass, although Laura planned to add a small fence in the course of time.

"The drinks are on the table." She waved a hand at a frosty pitcher standing nearby. "Neil and Laura Abbott, this is Greta Hobbs and the Lanes, Mark and Jeannie. Greta's husband isn't with us tonight."

"That's a nice way of saying he's out shacking up," Greta informed them bluntly. Laura decided at once that she didn't like this big-bosomed woman who looked both cheap and vulgar. She smiled nonetheless, and shook hands as warmly as she could manage.

The Lanes, however, she liked at once. Jeannie was about her own age, probably twenty, a delicately pretty blonde with wide and innocent eyes. Mark, her husband, had a comfortably collegiate manner, handsome in a pleasant, wholesome way. They looked, she thought, like the ideal young married couple, sweet and loving.

"I'm pleased to meet you," she greeted them with genuine relief. Her impressions of the other neighbors had not been altogether flattering, and it was a comfort to know that not all of the people around them were the same jaded, bitter sort.

She shook hands, too, with Hank Blair, and revised her opinion of him somewhat. It was easy to believe that he was as amoral as his wife had suggested. Seeing him at closer range, one could not overlook the aura of dissipation about him, despite his massive build and robust appearance. When he looked her over, she felt as though her clothes were being removed piece by piece, causing her to shiver involuntarily.

"It gets a little cool out here in the evenings," Hank said, although his smile hinted that he knew the real reason for her reaction. "Better warm yourself up with a martini."

"Thank you, I think I will," Laura answered. For once she felt as though a drink would be welcome.

Notwithstanding her impression that these people were not really her cup of tea, Laura soon found herself relaxing. Entertaining, she decided, was done on a very casual scale here. Hank took the emptied pitcher into the kitchen to refill it, and he kept an eye on the food already on the grill. Other than that, the guests were on their own, free to relax as they choose.

Neil had resumed his heavy drinking, but he continued to hold it well and Laura ceased worrying about being embarrassed by his behavior.

The drink helped her own mood, and she found herself enjoying the company of their neighbors. After all, these people certainly had gone out of their way to make them a part of the group. *I'll have to stop being a hick,* Laura told herself.

Life in Los Angeles was bound to be quite different from that in Terre Haute, and she simply must not be shocked by every outspoken statement made to her. Besides, for all she knew, Eve Blair had only been joking earlier. The evening was progressing without any threat of incident.

"I think I'll go powder my nose," she said to Eve, standing from the chaise longue.

"Use ours," Eve told her, waving a hand in the general direction of her house. "It's closer."

"I guess you're right," Laura agreed, and made her way to the back door. She realized that she was walking a little unsteadily—the martini had affected her more than she had realized—and she promised herself not to drink any more before dinner.

She was surprised, when she came back into the kitchen a few minutes later, to find Hank Blair standing in the doorway smoking a cigarette.

"Did I tell you I'm glad you moved in here?" he asked as she came into the room.

Laura hesitated. He stood in such a way that he partially blocked the doorway. Unless he moved, she could not pass him without making bodily contact. The thought was somehow unpleasant, and she wondered if she were afraid of him—or of herself. She knew instinctively that, once a woman admitted to herself he was attractive, it would be all but impossible to resist him.

"I—I'm glad I'm here," she answered, taking a step closer. She reminded herself that she was a married woman, that her husband was sitting only a few feet away, outside the door. Certainly she was not going to engage in a flirtation with this man, nor was he likely to attempt such a thing under such open circumstances. People did not flaunt their interest in daylight, not even fading daylight.

She was mistaken, however. Hank Blair reached out as she came nearer and, before she had time to step back, she was in his embrace. Her heart pounded as she felt his body crushing against hers. Here was a man, bigger and stronger even than Neil, a man of bold and flaming passions—a man who could satisfy the hungry desire that welled up within her.

He bent to kiss her and for an instant she turned her face upward toward him, ready for the kiss.

"No!" She came to her senses abruptly, turning her head away. "Let me go!" she whispered, fearful of being overheard by those outside. "How dare you?"

He said nothing, but his expression could only be described as a smirk. She knew he had felt the response in her body. He had guessed that she was tempted almost beyond the point of control. His arms held her for a moment longer before he released her. Breathing heavily, she darted through the door before he could seize her again.

No one seemed aware that she had been gone and returned. Neil was seated across the patio, his back to her, busily discussing something or another with Mark Lane. Greta Hobbs stood alone, staring toward the ocean into which the red sun was quietly sinking. Jeannie was watching her husband's face with unashamed affection.

Only Eve Blair was aware of her return. She glanced up as Laura descended the steps to the patio and Laura thought she saw a flicker of a smile cross the lovely face, but it was gone in a twinkling. Behind her, she heard the door open as Hank came out. Instinctively, she moved away, returning to the seat she had vacated earlier.

I won't let this spoil my evening, she told herself firmly, fighting off the mood of depression that threatened to engulf her. Hank Blair had made a pass—but she had been forewarned that he was a wolf. She had, after all, met one or two wolves before and knew that most were harmless unless encouraged. She had no intention of encouraging Hank Blair. She had made it clear to him that she wasn't the sort, and she was confident that the incident would not be repeated. She closed her eyes and leaned back.

A hand touched her bare leg a few minutes later and she jumped to a sitting position, startled by the touch. It was not Hank, however, but Eve Blair whose hand was resting on her leg.

"Heavens, you're a touchy one, aren't you?" the brunette said, her voice low. "I only wanted to tell you the food's almost ready."

"Thanks," Laura said, but the hand remained on her leg. She remembered the look Eve had given her earlier in the day and nervously moved away from her touch. "I'm starving."

She looked around and saw that Neil had left the Lanes and was now with Greta. To her dismay, they were showing every evidence of mutual interest. Neil's arm was about Greta's waist and she stood so close that her bulging breasts were flattened against his chest.

Laura realized he was drunk. By all rights she should take him home before trouble developed. But it would be rude of them to leave before eating the food that had been prepared for them.

It was Eve who interrupted the scene. "Hey you two," she called to them, with no attempt at discretion. "There's two bedrooms inside. It looks disgusting out here."

Greta shot her an unpleasant look. Far from being embarrassed, Neil laughed aloud at the remark and gave Greta's fleshy rear a friendly pat before moving slightly away from her. Laura considered again whether she should suggest leaving without waiting for the meal, but Eve was steering her firmly toward the table on which the food had been laid out.

Laura's anxiety increased as Neil declined food and continued to drink. By the time she had picked over her own meal, Laura knew she would have to suggest to him that they leave. She waited until Greta disappeared inside the house before deciding to approach him. Her attempt, however, was thwarted by Eve, who appeared at her side with a wedge of freshly-baked pie.

"I'm stuffed," Laura protested meekly, but Eve would not be discouraged.

"I spent half the afternoon baking that," she insisted.

"And in your honor. Force yourself."

When she looked in his direction again, Laura saw that Neil had moved from where he had been sitting. She turned in time to see him disappear inside the house.

He had followed Greta Hobbs inside. He was drunk enough to-have forgotten his true situation—or perhaps drunk enough to make another attempt. Laura sat in dismay for a moment, wondering what she should do. Should she ignore it, pretend she hadn't noticed? Or go home alone?

No! she thought firmly, standing, *he's my husband and I won't have this sort of thing happening.* She moved toward the door through which Greta and her husband had both gone, but Eve's voice stopped her.

"I wouldn't," she said in a low tone.

Laura turned around, blushing. "Surely you don't think...."

"I know Greta," Eve said bluntly.

Laura stood speechless, embarrassed because the others had noticed. Jeannie and Mark were staring at her across the patio. Hank Blair was watching her with a smug grin on his face.

Humiliated and angry, Laura sat down. If she left now or went inside, she would be admitting that what they suspected was the truth. For all she knew, nothing out of the way was going on inside.

As if to refute this thought, there was a burst of female laughter from inside—not pleasant, but raucous, derisive and mocking. It was followed by a loud oath.

They all stood up as Greta stormed out of the door, one hand holding her cheek. "The son of a bitch hit me!" she swore loudly, and went by them all without any more explanation, heading for her own house.

A moment later Neil burst through the door. His face was flushed with anger and what Laura knew was shame.

"Neil," she said, trying to stand in his way, but he shoved past her without even a glance and strode silently across the patio. The back door of their house slammed after him.

Laura wished that she could die rather than experience such a scene. Both Blairs were watching her with sardonic smiles, for which she hated them. Jeannie and Mark, who looked sympathetic and sorry for her, did not seem at all surprised by what had happened.

With a mumbled "Good night," Laura followed her husband across the grass that separated the two patios and into the house.

Neil was sprawled face down across the bed. He refused to meet her angry gaze.

"I had to try," he told her quietly. "I had to see if I could do it. I thought maybe the liquor...."

"You might have tried with me," she snapped, not caring if she hurt him.

He turned angry again, sitting up abruptly. "Hell, you were too busy in the kitchen with Hank Blair to worry about me. Do you think I didn't know what was going on?"

"You don't know what you're saying," she answered,

but she felt her face turn crimson.

"Can you honestly say nothing happened in there with him?" Neil accused her unmercifully.

Laura shrank from his anger. Of course she couldn't say that nothing had happened. But what could she say?

"You think I don't know that he's a man, and I'm not?!" Neil shouted, standing unsteadily in front of her. "Go on, admit it. He's got what you want. I can't give it to you, so you'd like to get it from him, wouldn't you."

Laura was crying despite her efforts to control herself. There was no answer she could give him. It was true, she *had* wanted the physical relief that Hank Blair had offered.

Her silence was all the answer that was necessary.

Neil rushed past her. The front door banged loudly after him. A moment later the car started up in the driveway. She listened as it roared away and faded into the distance. Finally, she began to undress for bed. It was her wedding night, but there was no one waiting in the bed for her. She felt alone and helpless.

CHAPTER FIVE

Laura awoke later than usual the next morning. She remained in bed, listening to sounds from the bathroom that told her Neil was already up and preparing for work.

It had been a disappointment to them that he had been unable to take more than one day off from work, due to the weeks that he had been off while in the hospital. Now, with the memory of the previous night's scene still fresh in her mind, she was actually grateful that he had to go to work. Perhaps it would be easier for them to face each other in the evening, after a day apart. Certainly she did not feel that she could face Neil just then.

She closed her eyes when he came back into the bedroom, pretending she was still asleep. She heard him pause once beside the bed and waited tensely to see if he would "awaken" her. He did not, and a short time later she heard him leave the house.

Not until she heard the car pull out of the driveway and move away down the street did she get up from the bed. She slipped into her robe and made her way to the kitchen, where the coffee Neil had brewed was still warm in the pot.

She sat there sipping her coffee and thought back to the afternoon and evening before, reliving the day in brief glimpses.

It had been a mistake, after all, to marry Neil. If their love had been more genuine, things might have been different for them. But she had approached the marriage with nothing more than a childish infatuation, and in the end she had married him more out of pity than from any other emotion, wanting not to hurt him more than he had already been.

It had been hopelessly unrealistic of her. She could see it was inevitable that she should hurt him all the more deeply. It was small wonder that he had devoted their wedding day to drinking himself blind.

But she was still at a loss to know what she should do. Was there any hope for their marriage? Was there any hope for Neil? He had really told her very little. Perhaps the loss of his virility was only temporary, although he had not said so. Certainly she owed it to him, and to herself, to give him every chance.

She wished desperately that there were someone to whom she could talk, if only for the sake of company. She knew no one but her new neighbors. She could obviously not talk to Greta. She would be just as happy were she never to see that woman again. Nor was Eve Blair likely to offer much comfort. At most, Eve would be cynically amused by the situation.

She thought of Jeannie Lane. Young though the girl was, she seemed to be intelligent, and she alone of the women had been sympathetic during yesterday's embarrassing scene.

Suddenly eager for someone else's company, Laura decided to walk over to the white house she knew was Jeannie's. If nothing else, perhaps they could have coffee together and a few minutes of idle chatter. Even that prospect was cheering.

Dressed, Laura left her kitchen and made her way across the patio, circling about the patio of the Blair home, half expecting as she did so that Eve Blair would intercept her. There was no sign of Eve, however, and Laura approached the Lane house without incident.

As she neared the back door of the trim, white house, she heard the sound of voices. She was at the door itself before she saw through the screen that Jeannie already had company. Eve Blair was in the kitchen, standing with her back to the open window.

Laura hesitated. She did not particularly feel in the mood for Eve's cynicism this morning. On the other hand, if she turned around and started toward home, she might be seen leaving and that would appear all the more rude.

It was not her intention to eavesdrop, but she could not help overhearing. The voices carried clearly through the open door and window. Laura remained, listening despite herself.

"I've told you before, Eve, the answer is no." Jeannie's voice was pleasant, but firm and edged with anger.

"What are you, a professional virgin?" Eve spoke in a harsh, cutting tone—

Laura blushed, realizing that the conversation was indeed personal, clearly one she should not hear. She undoubtedly should leave before she heard anything further from inside.

"I'm married," Jeannie argued. "And even if I weren't, the answer would be the same. I'm sorry, but it's just not my cup of tea."

Eve's immediate reaction was a derisive snort.

"All right, have it your way, little Red Riding Hood. But one of these days you'll get bored with that husband of yours, and you'll see things my way. I've met your type before."

"Don't count on it."

There was a pause before Jeannie snapped: "I told you not to do that!"

Eve chuckled and her tone became lower and more sultry. "I still think you're faking. Any woman would like that, regardless of who did it. I'll bet that sexy Mrs. Abbott wouldn't push me away."

Laura felt her cheeks burning. It was all too clear to her what was happening inside the kitchen. She had not been mistaken when she suspected that Eve Blair's interest in her extended below and beyond the call of ordinary friendship. As, obviously, she was not the only one in whom Eve took an interest.

"Well, hello."

Laura jumped at the sound of Eve's voice, and looked up to see the dark face peering through the screen door at her.

"Been here long?"

"No," Laura answered, not very convincingly. "I just walked up."

"Come in, why don't you," Jeannie suggested, appearing also at the door. "I've just made fresh coffee."

"I don't want to intrude," Laura protested. She knew her answer must sound rather foolish. Here she was, after all, at the doorstep.

"Oh I was just going," Eve told her, as though suspecting the reason for Laura's hesitation.

She opened the screen door, brushing intimately past Laura as she came out. "You two have fun together. Maybe I'll see you all later."

Laura looked after her briefly as Eve strode across the brick of the patio and disappeared within her own house. Then, remembering that Jeannie was still standing at the open door, Laura smiled up at her and stepped inside.

"I feel as though I owe everyone an apology for last night," Laura said, seating herself at the glass topped table.

Jeannie busied herself getting cups and pouring coffee. "Don't feel badly," she said over her shoulder. "We got pretty much the same initiation—when we moved in last month, except...." she checked herself before she finished the statement.

"Except that Mark didn't bite?" Laura finished the sentence for her.

Jeannie blushed and set the coffee on the table, seating herself across from Laura. "Mark's only a man, after all. I'm sure he was tempted—any man would be when it's thrown in his face like that. To tell you the truth, I stood on his feet when he tried to get up."

Laura smiled at the young woman's attempt to smooth things over.

"I wish it were that simple in my case."

"I know," Jeannie said simply. "Greta's not the sort to keep things to herself."

Laura had nothing to say to that. So they all knew the truth about Neil and herself and their marriage. What must they be saying? Not Jeannie, of course, nor Mark—they were too basically decent to derive pleasure from someone else's problem. But Eve and Hank must have found it amusing.

"I only wanted you to know," Jeannie explained, flashing an embarrassed smile. "I hate gossip behind someone's back. Come on, let's drink this coffee."

Laura was grateful for Jeannie's honesty as for the tactful change of subject. The matter did not come up again. Instead, they discussed the houses and Laura's plans for decorating. Jeannie had ideas for planting and landscaping, and suggested numerous flowers that would grow well.

"I'm afraid I'm at a loss on that subject," Laura admitted, more relaxed than earlier. Jeannie had been just the tonic she had needed.

"Don't worry about it. We'll go on a plant-shopping spree one of these days, and I'll show you what a busy-body I can be."

"You're nicer than some of the other neighbors," Laura said bluntly.

Jeannie grinned and dropped her eyes. "You mustn't think too badly of Eve," she said, although Laura had not mentioned anyone by name. "She's not a bad sort, even if she has some rather strange—ways. She can be very kind."

"I'm sure she can," Laura agreed without much conviction. It was difficult for her to imagine Eve being "kind" without some ulterior motive. She did not ask about the "strange ways" Jeannie referred to, nor mention that she had overheard the earlier conversation between the two.

Although her problems remained unsolved, Laura felt considerably better when she finally stood up to leave.

"Thanks for the company," she said, and meant it.

"Come over any time," Jeannie assured her, seeing her to the door. "My kitchen door's always open."

Laura glanced across toward her own house as she came out, and then at the Blairs'. She had the feeling that Eve Blair was watching, waiting for her to pass by on her way home. Instead, she turned impulsively toward the beach and the ocean. There was much that she should be doing at home, she knew, but her heart wasn't in it. She felt drawn to the beach, empty and tranquil.

Once on the sand, she removed her sandals and carried them with her as she walked aimlessly along, watching the water splash boldly up onto the beach then glide timidly back into itself.

She was not aware of Eve's presence until she heard

the voice behind her. "I'll bet you write poetry too."

Laura turned and forced a smile to her face.

"Nothing I'd want anyone to know about," she answered, continuing to walk along slowly. She half hoped that Eve would not follow, but Eve moved alongside and began to keep pace.

"Your husband...," Eve began, adding when she saw the instinctive withdrawal on Laura's part. "Now don't go getting your back up. In the first place, Greta spread it all around, so it's hardly a secret. In the second place, it just might do you some good to talk about it."

Laura sighed. She could not argue that point. She did want to talk about it to someone. Eve, after all, was obviously a woman of some experience. Perhaps in the long run she was just the one with whom to discuss the subject.

"It's not an easy subject," she said aloud.

"He can't? At all?" Eve's questions were typically short and blunt.

"No," Laura admitted simply.

"Too bad. Especially for a young, pretty thing like you."

Laura remembered the remark she had overheard earlier about herself. Was Eve making a pass at her now?

"It's not all that terrible," she argued.

Eve laughed softly. "I suppose you're going to tell me you don't like sex."

"I didn't say that," Laura answered impulsively, then regretted the words. She felt she must sound as if she were bursting at the seams. No matter what she said to Eve, it seemed always to be the wrong thing.

"Anyway," she added. "I'm not the only one with problems, from what I've seen."

It was a malicious thing to say, she knew, but she wanted very much to change the subject. She had been mistaken to think she could expect any reasonable suggestion from Eve.

The remark seemed not to perturb Eve at all. "Hank and I? There's no secret about that either. Aside from the facts that he's great in bed and makes good money, he's pretty worthless."

"Then why on earth...?"

"Did I marry him? That's not very mysterious either. I lived in a jerkwater town. His company sent him there for a year. He looked like the best chance I had to escape, so I took full advantage of the opportunity. I gave him a good time, the best he could hope for there, and then I announced to Mama and Papa that I was about to become a mother. They did the rest for me. I'll have to give old Hank credit, he went along with it nobly."

"Didn't you care for each other at all?" it seemed impossible to Laura that two people could marry for such unromantic reasons. Even she and Neil had been infatuated with one another.

"Oh, we get along together fine, which is the important thing. We both like a good time, and we both like to get our fun wherever we can. I don't bother him, and he doesn't bother me. He needed a wife anyway for business purposes, and I can be charming when it's called for. Half of his success is due to the fact that his boss likes me—preferably on my back."

Laura decided that she would believe almost anything about Eve Blair, but she left her thoughts unspoken.

"Like I said," Eve went on, dropping one hand lightly about Laura's shoulders. "Hank has some assets. He *is* good in bed. He went for you, you know. Maybe you should let him fix you up."

Laura moved away from the arm, annoyed and shocked by the suggestion.

"For your information," she said, not caring whether she offended or not. "I don't need anyone to make arrangements for me. I certainly am not going to carry on with another woman's husband, not even with her blessing."

Eve shrugged, but her smile seemed to indicate that she was more amused than offended. "Just a suggestion, that's all. Of course, there are other solutions, you know."

"Such as sleeping with the other woman?" Laura asked angrily.

Eve's smile became a laugh. "So you *were* eavesdropping this morning! It doesn't matter, really. I'd have brought it up sometime, anyway. Besides, it's not such a bad idea, don't you agree?"

"I couldn't agree with you less." Laura turned quickly about, walking back toward the houses. Eve went right along with her, not in the least perturbed by Laura's obvious anger.

"Look at it reasonably." Eve pursued the subject. "It's not as though you were breaking your marriage vows, whatever they may be worth in your case. You wouldn't be sleeping with another man."

She pulled at Laura's arm, bringing them both to an abrupt stop. "Have you ever been kissed by another woman?"

Laura shook her head, more frightened than angry. Their eyes met, and she felt the shock wave of the other woman's personality, strong and demanding, threatening to engulf her.

Eve pulled her closer, and Laura yielded weakly. So much had happened to arouse the desires of her body, and there had seemed to be no way to fulfill those desires. Nor was there likely to be, at least not with Neil. And here before her was a beautiful, fascinating creature who was blatantly offering her relief. It was strange and unreal, yet Laura felt herself responding to Eve's touch, moving helplessly in her encircling arms.

She was painfully aware of Eve's closeness, of her heady beauty, like an unfamiliar, exotic flower. She could smell Eve's perfume, strong and intoxicating, mingled with the clean, animal scent of Eve's body.

"We'll be seen," she whispered, aware that it was not the denial she had intended to make. She wanted to say that she wasn't interested, that such a situation sickened her.

"Not a chance," Eve told her softly, her voice no more than a silken whisper. "Not even Jeannie could see us way out here, and there are no houses the other way."

There was no time for further protest. Laura felt the touch of lips against hers, lips that were sweet, moist and demanding. The fiery tip of Eve's tongue parted her lips, seeking her tongue. To her amazement, she responded to the kiss, her tongue hungrily answering the call.

The kiss was long and ardent. When Laura opened her eyes again, she saw Eve's eyes mocking her, confident of success.

"No!" Laura managed to gasp breathlessly.

Eve offered no struggle when she pulled away. Laura turned and ran, frightened at what was happening to her. She remembered that she had dropped her shoes somewhere back there in the sand, but she dared not go back for them. Eve would be there, waiting to torture her still further.

She ran on blindly until she had stumbled up the steps into the safety of her own kitchen and closed the door after herself.

CHAPTER SIX

Laura remained inside the rest of the day, not daring to see Eve again. She feared Eve might come over but, as the day passed and there was no evidence of her neighbor, her fears finally dwindled somewhat, although she remained depressed and confused by what had happened.

She told herself again and again that she was not weak, that she could not be victimized by Eve's glossy sophistication. Even if the potential for a lesbian relationship lay within her, it had never expressed itself before, nor did it of necessity have to be expressed now. Eve had caught her at an exceptionally weak moment. At another time she would never have responded as she had to Eve's kiss. Even so, she had summoned up the strength necessary to escape the temptation.

But, she found herself replying each time, it *had* been a temptation, it *had* been necessary to run away. One moment longer and she might have surrendered to Eve's demands. The thought was enough to make her shudder and promise herself that in the future she would avoid being alone with Eve.

Neil arrived home late in the evening. There was

no need to ask what had delayed him. It was obvious that he had spent the time drinking, although she was not experienced enough to know how much he had consumed.

It was obvious, too, that his mood was anything but cheerful. He avoided her attempt to greet him with a kiss, brushed by her with a mumbled "Hello," and made his way into the bedroom to change clothes. When he emerged a few minutes later, he went directly to the bar.

Laura concealed her disappointment as best she could. There was much that had to be discussed between them, but she decided it was best to wait until Neil was sober again. She wondered when that might be. She hoped his binge would not continue for long. He had never been a heavy drinker, but his accident might have changed all that.

Neil sat alone in the living room, drinking, while she prepared dinner. He brought his glass with him to the table when she served the meal. She noticed that he drank far more than he ate but refrained from making an issue of it.

After dinner she stacked the dishes in the sink, promised herself she'd do them later in the evening and joined her husband in the living room.

Neil sat on the sofa, with still another drink in his hand. Uncertain of her reception she crossed the room and sat near him on the sofa.

"I'm sorry, Neil," she said gently.

The face he turned to her was so filled with bitterness and anger that she scarcely recognized the man she had married.

"You're sorry!" He spat the words at her. "What did you think it would be, a bed of roses? Did you think I'd hire a couple of studs to take care of you while I sat back and watched the show?"

The words stung. She bit her lip to hold back the tears.

"We can have the marriage annulled," she suggested as calmly as she was able.

"Oh, sure," he snapped viciously. "Tell the whole world that Neil Abbott isn't a man anymore! Why don't you hire a publicity agent? Maybe you can get it in the headlines while you're at it!"

She began to cry, her face in her hands. After a moment she felt his arm around her, pulling her toward him.

"I'm sorry, baby," he whispered. "I should never have let you marry me when we both knew it couldn't work."

His breath was strong with liquor, and his actions clumsy and rough. Laura sat rigid as he fumbled awkwardly with her blouse, tearing loose some of the buttons when they resisted his efforts to undo them. His hand slid inside.

He swore as the bra, too, resisted his clumsy efforts. He ripped it fiercely aside, mauling her tender breasts with his powerful hands.

Laura felt her nipples spring to vibrant life at the touch. Her entire body suddenly quaked with desire.

Not again! she thought in anguish as her ardor began to mount with feverish rapidity. *I can't endure being aroused again, without....*

She thought of Eve on the beach that morning, the soft, sweet lips against hers. She had never before imagined herself in such a situation, yet she had heard that there were ways for two women....

"There are other ways," she said in Neil's ear, before she took time to consider the words.

Neil stiffened. His hands froze on the flesh of her breasts.

"What do you mean?" he asked hoarsely.

"There are other things we could do...."

He pushed her roughly away from him.

"What in the hell do you think I am, some kind of sexual pervert?"

"It isn't perverted," she sobbed, crying openly. "I've read books. Married couples do things together. It's all right."

"Not for me it isn't!" he shouted. "When I want a woman, I want her my way—the right way. It'll be the right way or not at all—and that goes for both of us, my hot little wife!"

He stood, swaying unsteadily, and staggered the bar for a fresh drink. Laura stared after him in frustration. Then she ran into the bedroom and threw herself across the bed, giving herself up to tears of anguish.

Her crying dwindled, finally, and ended. She rose, changed her blouse for a fresh one and returned to the living room. She found Neil asleep on the sofa.

More likely, she thought with bitterness, *he's passed out from all the liquor.* She went by him without stopping, out the back door into the cool night air.

What was she to do now? Neil would not consent to any substitutes for sexual intercourse. At least in that way they might have compensated, relieved some of the pressure of their unfortunate marriage. But even that door was closed to her.

He had refused to consider an annulment as well. She could fight him on that, although she knew little about the laws involved. But how much ugliness and humiliation would they both have to suffer? It would be hard enough for her, but ever so much worse for Neil. Once again, she decided to sacrifice her happiness for Neil's. She shivered involuntarily as she thought of what that would mean in the weeks and months before them.

"It gets cool here at night." Eve's voice startled her, coming unexpectedly from the darkness.

Laura turned in the direction of the Blair home. Eve was seated on a chaise lounge, barely visible in the darkness of the patio.

"I wasn't planning to stay out here," Laura told her, peering at the vague figure of her neighbor. Even in the darkness, with distance between them, she could feel the woman's attraction.

"You certainly can't go back in there and continue that battle—or has he passed out by now?"

"Does sound carry that well here?"

Eve chuckled. "I'm afraid it does, at least between your house and mine. The others aren't quite so close together."

Laura wondered what she should do. Neil had passed out, but there was no guarantee he wouldn't awaken and start a new quarrel. She could not help being frightened by Eve's magnetism and yet the woman did offer companionship she needed very much at the moment. Staying outside, even with Eve, was preferable to more of Neil's brutality.

"Hank's not home," Eve said, playing upon Laura's hesitation.' "Why don't we keep each other company for a while?"

"Thanks," Laura answered, resigning herself to the situation and moving across the patio.

As she moved closer, she saw that Eve was wearing only a skimpy pair of shorts and a halter. In the pale moonlight, the lithe body seemed to be molded of bronze.

"Sit here," Eve directed, making room for Laura on the lounge.

Although she feared what might happen, Laura did as she was told, feeling a giddy excitement as her body touched Eve's long, slender legs.

"Your trouble is you're too sensitive," Eve told her. One gentle hand reached out to stroke Laura's hand softly. "Me, I don't let anything bother me. That's the only way to get along with any man."

Laura said nothing, afraid to speak. Her entire body was tingling with sexual desire her husband had aroused in her. Her breasts were still warm from his touch.

She knew that she should protest when Eve pulled her closer, but she made no sound except for her labored breathing. And when the dark, lovely face poised over hers, she could only wait helplessly for Eve's kiss.

At the touch of Eve's mouth, she knew that she would not be able to refuse anything this woman asked. She was weak from tension and quarrelling, too aroused sexually and in need of satisfaction to resist the demands that Eve was making.

Skilled hands found the buttons of her blouse and one by one undid them. Laura remembered Neil's roughness and crudity. Eve's movements were gentle and reassuring.

She had not replaced the bra Neil had ripped. Nothing protected her heaving breasts from the eager exploration. And she was glad. Her nipples were hot with passion, rigid and trembling as the long, soft fingers played upon them, fondling, stroking, gently pressing.

Laura gasped as one ruby tip was sucked into an eager mouth, and all fear vanished, replaced with a raging desire for release. It no longer mattered that it was not Neil, was not even a man. She had to be satisfied, in any way, by anyone.

"Don't be afraid," Eve whispered into the darkness. "I'll be good to you, sweetheart."

"Not here," Laura protested feebly. What if Neil should awaken and come looking for her? But she could not move away from the glorious pleasure of the mouth that was ravishing her quivering breasts, nor the hands that were exploring the softness of her legs.

"There's no one to see," Eve told her. "Jeannie and Mark are out for the evening. Hank's not home. Your husband is dead to the world. I want you here, now, with all the stars in heaven watching me love you."

Laura could not answer. She was panting with excitement. Her thighs seemed to melt at the touch of the hot fingers upon them. Her body reacted as if of its own accord, opening itself hungrily to the search.

She was falling backward, drifting on the lounge. Nothing mattered now but the hands, becoming more ardent, more demanding with each passing second and the mouth that explored her body with ever-increasing boldness.

"That's it, baby. Easy now," Eve crooned. She was a virtuoso and Laura's body was the instrument on which she played her serenade of love.

Each touch, each motion, skillfully increased their frenzied ardor. The consuming fire of youthful passion blazed wildly within Laura's body. She writhed and thrashed, no longer able to keep her body still, no longer able even to think. She could do nothing but surrender herself to delight and happiness that became almost unbearable.

"Oh, I can't stand it," she groaned aloud, oblivious now to the danger of being heard or seen. "It's too sweet, too wonderful!"

Eve was merciless. Time and again she brought Laura to the verge of completion, only to lead her gently back. Each peak soared higher than the last, until Laura became nothing more than a raging animal, mad with lust, lost in a paradise of physical pleasure.

Laura could not contain the cry that burst from her lips as her body erupted at last in a soul-shattering orgasm. She threw herself about frantically as Eve clung tightly to her. Again and again she moaned, while sensation ebbed slowly and sweetly from her.

She lay spent and exhausted as the world about her came gradually into focus. Eve found her cigarettes where they had fallen and lit two, handing one to Laura. Laura inhaled deeply, filling herself once more with reality.

"No wonder your husband is miserable," Eve said abruptly. "If he's ever had you, it must be hell not being able to have you again."

Laura stiffened, remembering who and where she was, and what she had just done.

She sat up, weakly restoring her clothes to a semblance of decency.

"I've got to go," she whispered, overcome with shame and anger.

"Don't," Eve pleaded, trying to hold her there. "Come inside. We can have hours—the whole night—together, if you like. I can teach you so much more, so many things you'll delight in learning."

Laura brushed away the hand that had returned to her breasts, although she had felt the excitement beginning anew within her body.

"I won't lie to you," she said, looking down at her reclining companion, "and say that I didn't enjoy what we just did together. It wasn't the way it was with Neil, but that was long ago, and there's been nothing for me since."

Eve reached for her again, taking the remark as encouragement. Laura shuddered, but forced herself to push the hand away again.

"But it can't happen again," she finished. "Don't even try."

"I won't have to," Eve replied with a sardonic smile. "Next time, *you'll* ask *me*. I've been through this before. I know your type. You'll tell yourself this was the only time, and you'll avoid me for a while. But the next time your husband gets you all hot and bothered you'll come crawling back to little Eve for happiness. I can afford to wait. After all, I can get mine lots of places, any time I want it. You can't."

Laura tried to outstare her, but she was no match for the stubborn conviction she saw in Eve's eyes. Without answering, Laura turned and hurried through the darkness to her own house, Eve's prophecy ringing in her ears.

Was she right? Would it be that way? She had wanted to tell Eve she was wrong, but she did not feel at all sure.

Neil was still asleep. Nothing had changed —except that she had just found sexual satisfaction with another woman. She had faced the fact that she could not live without sex, that her needs were stronger than she ever had imagined—and lost.

CHAPTER SEVEN

Laura did not pretend to sleep late in the morning. There was no longer any point in hoping that Neil would apologize, or that things would improve for them after a few short hours. She knew that no solution was going to spring from the woodwork, no magic spell would alter things to what they could have been.

She got up from the bed while Neil was in the bathroom and made her way into the kitchen, where she made coffee. She was still there when he left. He did not even come into the room for coffee or to tell her he was leaving. She told herself it was just as well— she was not up to a scene at the moment—and poured herself another cup of coffee, her third.

She felt sick whenever she remembered the previous night, remembering herself as the wild, lustful animal she had been. Was she truly so distraught by her situation that she was easy prey for anyone who desired her body?

She was not a lesbian, of that she was certain. And yet she had surrendered easily to Eve's lust. In the frenzy of her sexual need she had abandoned herself completely. It was all well and good to say that she would refuse when Eve tried again (and she was sure that Eve would try again). But would she really be able to refuse? And for how long?

How long would she be able to hold out without the normal sexual release that she so evidently and urgently needed? Even if Neil's condition were to improve, it would not happen all at once. For all she knew, it might be a matter of years, years in which her body would make its needs felt more and more urgently. Today she *might* be able to resist Eve's advances. But what of the morrow, or next week, or a month from then?

Despondently, she drank the strong coffee and tried to think of some way out of the nightmare trap into which she had fallen. She could, perhaps, return home for a visit, go away from a locale whose very air seemed charged with sex.

Surely, the time apart would give both Neil and herself opportunity to regain their perspectives. Given the freedom to think more clearly and without emotional pressures, they might find the solution for which they were seeking.

Neil might even reconsider his refusal to participate in substitute activities. After the previous evening, she could scarcely doubt that such substitution would prove satisfactory to her.

The trip was not as simple as that to decide upon, however. There was the question of money. The money she had left, which she had brought with her from Indiana, was scarcely enough to make a cross-country trip even one way. Nor was it likely that Neil, in his present frame of mind, would finance such a holiday, or condone it.

Her parents, of course, would respond to a call for help, but she knew that they could ill afford such extravagance. Anyway, she couldn't ask it of them. She could not help but feel that it was she who had gotten herself into this situation and should solve it for herself. If only she knew how!

The day passed quietly and uneventfully. Laura remained inside the house, attending to the housework. There was shopping to be done, but tomorrow was Saturday and she would have the car—if Neil was not out.

More than once, she thought of going to the beach, but the prospect of Eve's following her was too likely. She did not feel up to another encounter with the dark-haired vixen. As it was, she expected Eve to knock at the door any time throughout the day to badger her still further. She did not, however, and the day passed quietly, if not pleasantly.

Neil did not return home when he should have. Laura told herself unhappily that he was drinking again. She left her stew to simmer slowly and settled down with a book. Her attention, however, Would not remain on the pages. She kept remembering her experience with Eve the night before. Despite her better judgment, she could not help but feel resurgent desire for the same sort of physical pleasure. She felt the pull of Eve's attraction even in her own living room.

She closed her book finally, unable to remember a

single word she had read, and lit a cigarette, glancing at her watch as she did so. It was after eight o'clock. Neil should have been home by six at the latest.

By nine o'clock, her nerves were raw with worry and loneliness. She ate by herself, without much appetite. Afterward, she tried to watch television. That was no more successful than the book.

It was after ten o'clock when Neil finally returned home. She knew from his noisy entrance that he was drunk beyond control. He staggered into the bedroom, where she was preparing for bed, and stood swaying clumsily in the doorway.

Instinctively, Laura reached for a robe to conceal her waist-up nudity.

"Hey, don't cover up, sweetheart," he shouted loudly, leering at the flesh exposed before him, "I may want to use them."

"You're drunk, Neil," she told him, trying to remain calm, although inwardly she was seething with frustration and disappointment. She was also afraid of him. She could still remember his brutality of the previous evening. As drunk as he was now, there was no telling how cruel he might be. "Let me fix you some coffee."

"That isn't what I need," he told her. He came into the room, staggering toward her as he shrugged off his jacket and tie.

"It's no use," she told him, backing away. She bumped into the dresser and stopped. There was nowhere else to go. "You know it won't accomplish anything."

"That's what I like, a wife with faith in me."

Her remark, however, seemed to stop him. He stood in the center of the room. Laura breathed a sigh of relief as he began to undress himself, presumably for bed. His clothes fell to the floor about him in a careless heap.

Watching as his body was revealed. Laura could not help but experience a new wave of bitter anguish. He was such a handsome example of manly perfection, the ideal that every girl dreamed of. If only...but she left the thought unfinished.

He tore away the last shred of his clothing and looked up to see her watching him.

"Pretty good, huh?" he wanted to know, turning so that she could admire the flex and play of his muscles. "Quite a man, huh?"

"We'd better go to bed," she said quietly, frightened again as his eyes swept over her own nearly naked body. She moved in the direction of the king-sized bed, hoping that her coldness would chill the desire in his eyes.

"Now there's a first-class idea," he snickered. He moved with a speed she would not have thought possible for anyone as drunk as he, catching her in his huge arms.

"I'm gonna take my wife to bed," he declared. His strong hands clawed savagely at her body. The last of her clothing was torn away with a sudden ripping of silk.

"Neil, you're hurting me!" she protested, struggling to free herself from his iron grip.

"You're damned right I'm hurting you," he snarled viciously.

He lilted her easily from the floor and all but threw her across the bed. She tried to roll away, but he was too quick for that. He was upon her in an instant, his massive weight crushing the breath from her body.

"I can do it." he told her, clawing mercilessly at her naked thighs.

Through her fear, a glimmer of hope sprang into Laura's thoughts. Maybe he *could* do it. Maybe this was what he needed, enough frustration, enough anger, to trigger some animal response from within. If that were so, it was worth the bruises he was inflicting, worth being mauled by him.

"Yes," she said as she ceased struggling. "Yes, Neil, show me that you can."

She was ready for him, open to his thrust, eager, thrilled at the prospect of once again finding happiness with this fiery man. It would be as before, the total joy Neil had given her in the past.

He labored on and on, and slowly her hope began to die. It was useless. She had only fooled herself into thinking some miracle could change everything for them. She grew limp in his grasp.

Neil cursed bitterly, rolling away from her, and she knew without looking that he was crying. Full of pity for him, Laura managed to pull herself upright. Her body ached with disappointment.

"Neil," she whispered, reaching for him.

"Damn you!" he snarled, his eyes flashing with fury.

"Damn you!"

He struck out, his hand slapping her cheek. Laura reeled from the force of the blow and fell back away from him.

The bathroom door slammed after him.

Laura sat for a moment, dazed. Then, terrified beyond reason, she grabbed her robe from the chair and, donning it as she went, ran out of the house and into the night. She had to get away from him, had to turn to someone. And there was only one person to whom she could turn at the moment.

If Eve Blair was surprised to find her at the door, she gave no evidence of the fact.

"Come on in," she said casually, as though she had expected the visit.

Eve led her into the living room. Hank Blair was there, too, seated in front of the television set. He stood as Laura came into the room and turned off the television.

"Another bad night?" Eve asked, indicating a chair for Laura.

Self-consciously, Laura glanced in Hank's direction. He was staring at her with unconcealed interest and she remembered that the skimpy robe she was wearing did little to conceal her nudity.

"Don't be silly," Eve told her, interpreting the glance. "Hank knows all about everything. Don't let his being here frighten you."

Laura wondered if Hank knew about last night on the patio, but she could not bring herself to ask. She could not trust her voice.

"Why don't you take a walk, Hank," Eve suggested to her husband, "I think she needs a little comforting."

The smile that Hank flashed in her direction was unmistakable.

"Maybe I should stay around," he offered. "I might have just the sort of comfort she needs."

Laura flushed crimson. They were discussing her as though she were a piece of merchandise. She almost expected them to toss a coin to decide who would stay with her and who would leave.

"Some other time, maybe," Eve said firmly.

Hank still smiled, but he yielded. He nodded to Laura and left the room. A minute later, the back door opened and closed, and he was gone.

"I shouldn't have come barging in like this," Laura apologized meekly. "I don't even know why I did."

"Don't you?" Eve was standing directly in front of her legs apart, hands on hips. Laura looked up into the smiling face.

Her body was churning with the desire Neil had aroused in her mere moments before. She had wanted him to succeed, she had wanted it desperately, and had been left empty and unsatisfied. But there was an outlet available to her, a conclusion to what Neil had started. And she had come directly here.

"Ask me." Eve's smile was cold and spiteful.

Laura remembered clearly what Eve had said the night before: "...the next time you'll ask me...."

"I've got to have it," Laura admitted, her voice

quavery and uncertain. "Please—can we...?"

Eve turned without a word and moved across the room. She paused at the door that Laura knew led into the bedroom, glanced back meaningfully. Meekly, Laura stood and followed her.

Eve undressed quickly, just as Neil had done a few minutes before, although her motions were perfectly calculated to arouse desire in the onlooker. Laura watched, mesmerized, her eyes feasting on the loveliness of Eve's lean, sultry body. The golden tan gave a rich luster to the flesh. The breasts stood pointed and firm, smaller than Laura's but taut and enticing. Her stomach was a flat plane that melted into golden thighs and an intoxicating patch of blackness.

Eve kicked off her panties and pirouetted slowly, with the tantalizing grace of a stripper. Then, her eyes glued to Laura's she came across the bedroom. Laura's robe slid to the floor with a soft rustling sound, and they faced one another, two beautiful naked creatures linked by a common bond, the frantic urge that was churning within them.

"I don't know what to do," Laura whispered hoarsely. She knew that this time it could be no one-sided affair.

"You'll learn," Eve assured her. She reached beyond Laura's shoulder, and the lights went out with a click. Laura's hand was clasped in Eve's, and she allowed herself to be led across the dark room, lowered gently to the soft, inviting surface of the bed.

Fear prevented her from responding at first. She lay quietly, feeling once again the exhilarating thrill as Eve's hands and mouth played upon her trembling body, skillfully tracing exotic patterns over her breasts, her stomach, down to her thighs. The darting tongue awakened her slowly but surely, urging her to ecstasy.

Eve's mouth returned to Laura's, searing her lips, and then it was gone. Laura felt the soft touch of twin breasts brushing her face. Timidly at first, then with an increasing boldness, she tasted their sweetness. It was all so new to her, so excitingly different from anything she had experienced or even imagined before. She remembered everything that Eve had done to her the night before, and suddenly nothing mattered but the getting and giving of that same intense joy all over again.

"Yes," Eve groaned as Laura seized her hips in a fierce embrace. "Take me—*that's right!*"

She continued to moan and gasp as Laura practiced still more of the art Eve had so ably taught her. The bed rocked as their bodies tumbled and tossed about.

"Oh yes, my darling, *yes!*" Eve cried aloud. She clawed wildly at Laura's hair as she gave herself up to a long and delirious climax.

They fell apart, panting from the exertion. Gasping for air, Laura stared upward at the dim whiteness of the ceiling. Yes, she had learned well.

CHAPTER EIGHT

It was at least an hour later when Hank returned from his walk. Laura heard the kitchen door and regretted that she had not left before he returned. She could not bear the thought of facing him, of seeing the knowing smirk on his handsome face. Why shouldn't he laugh at her? A short time ago she had refused his advances, had told him puritanically that she did not believe in that sort of thing. And here she was now, in his house, in his bed, with his wife.

She waited until she heard him enter the bathroom before she rose from the bed and found her robe. She avoided turning on the light. Eve sat up in the bed, and a match flared brightly as she lit a cigarette.

"How about a drink," she suggested from the bed. "I heard Hank come in."

"No thanks."' Laura replied without commenting on Hank's presence. She did not wait for Eve to argue the point but opened the bedroom door and hurried out. Hank was still in the bathroom, and she left the house quickly, running.

Neil was asleep atop the cover. Without waking him, Laura shed her robe and slid under the bedclothes to the far side of the bed. It was much later before she was able to fall asleep. Even then she slept fitfully....

* * * * * * *

Neil was still asleep when she awoke in the morning. It was Saturday, and he would not be going into the office. She bathed and dressed as quietly as possible, hoping that he would not awaken before she was ready. Without even taking time to prepare coffee, she took the car keys from the dresser where he had tossed them the night before, and left a note to tell him that she had gone shopping.

It was a relief to be away from the house. The bright sunlight poured through the windows of the car. The warm breeze ruffled her hair. She stopped for coffee at a small, virtually empty, coffee shop that overlooked the beach and the shimmering surface of the ocean. From the window she watched a group of teenagers playing together in the sand, happy young boys and girls. It seemed an eternity since she had been that young, that carefree. With a grimace, she turned away from the scene and left the restaurant, driving on to the supermarket.

It was impossible not to think of all that was happening to her. Her shopping was mechanical, her thoughts on her personal situation. Last night burned in her memory. She could not help but feel pity for Neil, despite his brutality. She had felt real anguish at his frustration the night before. He had been so certain of success. Was that a good sign? Had he come as close to accomplishment as he seemed to think?

She stopped in the middle of the aisle, staring at the rows of canned foods surrounding her. He had mentioned the name of his doctor to her. Carton, that was the name. Surely he was the one she should talk to. Perhaps even now, while Neil knew nothing about it.

She left her half-filled cart where it was and hurried outside to a telephone booth. Yes, there was a Doctor Carton listed in Santa Monica, only a few minutes away. Breathlessly she dialed the number.

"Yes," the girl who answered told her, the Doctor is in, but he has no open appointments for this morning."

"Oh please," Laura begged. "I must see him. Tell him I'm Neil Abbott's wife. I won't take more than a few minutes."

The girl returned to the phone a few minutes later to say that the Doctor would see her but that the visit had to be brief.

Laura left without finishing her shopping. Someone would find the cart and put the things away. There were more important items she had to attend to without any further delay....

* * * * * * *

Doctor Carton seemed surprised to learn that Neil Abbott was married.

"I understood he was a single man," he told her.

"We've only just been married," Laura explained, realizing how very foolish she must sound. "I wanted to ask you about—about his accident. Will Neil be *permanently* injured?"

The Doctor peered at her for a long while over the rims of his glasses. "You mean, is there any hope for your marriage?"

Laura nodded her head. "Yes, that's what I really want to know."

"I'm afraid not." He gave her a moment to consider that statement before he went on.

She understood little of what he was telling her. He explained at length about nerves, and muscular control. All that she really understood was that Neil would probably never recover from his injury.

"But if he felt that he could...?"

"Only an illusion, the result of an intense desire on his part. That is usual in cases of this sort. Your husband has lost his ability to function in a very important manner. It's difficult for even a strong mind to accept. There will be times when he's particularly aroused, or perhaps if he's been drinking, when he will be certain that he can perform after all. Don't let it fool you.

"No miracle will enable him to perform the sexual act again. Of course, you surely must realize that there are other ways, ways which would be quite possible for him, and would, I think, satisfy both of you to some degree."

Laura had no reply. She had already made a bid in that direction, a bid Neil had rejected.

Perhaps, in time—if there were time, if she could endure long enough.

She extended a hand toward the doctor. "Thank you

for your time. I had to know the truth about Neil."

She left the office in a daze. Neil had only imagined it the night before. He had been drunk and frustrated, and his crazed desire had played tricks on him, on both of them. But how could she bring herself to tell him that? Or was it better for the present to allow him to retain his illusions?

She stopped at another market on her way home and brought groceries for the next few days. As she drove into the driveway at home, she realized how much she had come to hate this house and Sandy Knoll. They had seemed so lovely to her before, so filled with promise for the future. Now they held nothing but unhappiness.

Neil was up when she came in, and for the first time since their wedding, he was sober. The drink in his hand this time was coffee, not liquor.

To her surprise, he jumped up to help her with the groceries, working quickly and quietly to help put things away in their proper places. She started out of the kitchen when they were finished, but he caught her arm.

"Laura," he said gently, his eyes pleading with her for understanding. "I'm sorry for everything that's happened between us."

"I guess we both are," she admitted, trying to smile. She could not, however, feel any real affection toward him, not just yet.

"Don't draw away from me," he begged when she started to leave again. "I have to tell you something. It's going to be all right."

She stared at him without understanding for a moment what he was saying.

"It'll be all right," he repeated. "Be patient, darling. Last night I...well, I almost did it. I'll be able to go all the way again, I know I will."

She looked away from the eagerness she saw in his eyes. His illusion had stayed with him. It had been so real to him that even sober and in the light of day, he still believed something had happened which could never happen. And she simply did not have the heart to tell him the truth.

He put his arm around her, drawing her closer to him. "Let's try again," he whispered. "Let's try now."

For a moment, she nearly surrendered. She wanted so badly to believe with him, to accept the dream as reality.

Realization of the brutal awakening that would follow brought her back to her senses.

"*No!*" She pulled away from him violently. Even if her refusal hurt him, she could not suffer that sort of torture again, not this morning. It would be easier for him to blame it on her refusal than to have him go through the shame of another failure—easier for both of them.

She saw the hurt in his eyes, but he did not try to hold her again. She was prevented the necessity of further comment by a soft knock on the back door.

Jeannie Lane was there. Laura thought of the conversation she had overheard between Jeannie and Eve. Jeannie had been strong enough to resist Eve's temptation. But then, she reminded herself, Jeannie did not have to look outside her marriage for sexual satisfaction. Would she have been as strong if Mark were incapable of performing the sex act with her?

"Sorry to be a bother," Jeannie apologized with a smile as she came into the kitchen, "but I wondered if you could do me a big favor. Mark's at the office today, and I just got a call from San Diego. My mother's sick, and she's all by herself. Do you suppose you could drive me into town so I could catch a bus?"

"Of course. It won't be any bother," Laura assured her quickly. She was grateful for another excuse to go out. It would prevent a fresh argument with Neil.

"Thanks ever so much," Jeannie answered, genuinely grateful. "I left a note for Mark. We'll go whenever it's convenient for you."

"Right now is fine," Laura said, not looking at Neil to see what his reaction would be.

"Well, looks like I caught everybody with one fell swoop!" Eve's voice called through the door. Without waiting for an invitation, she opened the door and came into the kitchen.

"I decided it was a perfect day for the beach, and I hate going swimming alone. Of course, Hank's willing, but he's such a bore at times. Do I have any volunteers?"

Jeannie smiled and shook her head. "Afraid I can't, and Laura's already committed herself to drive me into town. My mother's under the weather, and I'm going to take a bus down to San Diego."

Eve's smile might have meant almost anything, and Laura wondered what thoughts she was conjuring up about the friendship between herself and Jeannie.

"Too bad," Eve said, without any real regret. "How about you, handsome?"

Neil smiled wanly. Even in his depressed mood, he was susceptible to flattery.

"I guess I don't have much else to do," he admitted. "Maybe I'll take you up on the invitation."

Laura could not help but feel a sense of relief. Perhaps if he spent the rest of the morning on the beach, Neil would remain sober. It was even possible that things were beginning to work themselves out. Certainly he seemed apologetic enough, and was trying hard to be pleasant for a change.

"I won't be long," she told him, patting his arm with real affection.

"Oh." Jeannie paused as she started to follow Laura from the kitchen. "I forgot to bring my checkbook. Give me a minute to run and get it, will you?" She smiled apologetically and dashed out the back door.

"I'll go change into a swim suit," Neil said, leaving the room also. To Laura's disappointment, she found herself alone with Eve.

She indicated a chair, trying half-heartedly to be cordial.

"Might as well relax," she said, dropping into another chair herself.

"Things seem to be more pleasant this morning," Eve commented, accepting the invitation. "You know, there's really no reason for sex to ruin your marriage, when Hank and I are available to make up for his shortcomings."

"You know I could never go along with anything like that," Laura told her stubbornly. "I feel bad enough about what has happened with you. I certainly could not allow anything to happen with Hank!"

Eve shrugged. "Why not? He's pretty good. I can tell you that. And you certainly don't have to worry about my being jealous—at least not as long as you don't cut me out. As for Neil, if you think he'd object, we simply won't tell him about it—although I think I could convince him of a few things, if I tried."

Laura shook her head in genuine amazement. "You don't care about anything, do you? I really think you have no concept whatsoever of morality."

"I got rid of that nonsense a long time ago," Eve answered bitterly. "And anyway, who's kidding whom? You think your husband loves you, yet he doesn't want you to have physical pleasure and satisfaction that he can't provide. That's not love, that's pure selfishness. Hank and I both happen to need and enjoy a variety of experiences. What makes you think we care any less for one another because we admit that need and go along with it?"

Laura had no answer for her. Fortunately, she was spared by the return of Jeannie, running breathlessly across the patio and into the kitchen.

"All set," she announced cheerfully unaware of the tense currents flowing between the other two.

Relieved at the diversion, Laura rose from the chair, nodding politely to Eve as she started out.

"See you later at the beach?" Eve called as they went out.

"Maybe," Laura called back.

CHAPTER NINE

Despite the heavy Saturday traffic along the highway, it did not take long to drive Jeannie into town to the bus station. There was half an hour to go before the bus left. Laura waited with Jeannie in the coffee shop until time to leave, promising as she saw Jeannie to the bus, that she would keep an eye on Mark.

"He's so helpless," Jeannie told her as she started up the bus' steps. "He can't even boil an egg for himself. I'm appointing you to nag him in my absence."

Laura laughed at that. "Don't worry about a thing," she insisted firmly.

She waved good-bye as the bus pulled away, watching Jeannie's window-framed face disappear in the distance. Then, abandoning the gaiety she had feigned for Jeannie's benefit, she returned to her car and started off for home, once more reflecting upon her situation with Neil.

The hope that had glimmered within her a short time before had already begun to dim. It was true enough that Neil had been sober this morning, and genuinely apologetic toward her. His illusions regarding his capabilities, however, had persisted, as had his determination to try again.

Even if Neil were gradually regaining control of his emotions, there was still little likelihood that they could solve the problems that faced them. He was no more capable of sexual intercourse when sober than when he was drunk.

Somehow he had to be made to face the truth. His reaction would be bitter, perhaps violent. She had seen that he was capable of violence. There was no telling how far he would go.

She arrived home to find the house empty and quiet. Neil, apparently, was still with Eve and Hank at the beach. She thought about joining them. She would have to eventually, if only for the sake of maintaining the uneasy peace between Neil and herself. For the moment, however, she wanted nothing so much as to relax alone.

She poured herself a glass of lemonade from the pitcher in the refrigerator and went out the back door, dropping wearily into the canvas chair on the patio.

She glanced around the small patio. There was so much she had planned to do here to make the area more enjoyable. She would have liked to have a grille like the Blairs', and she had planned a small fence, with perhaps some shrubs to give a little privacy. It was unlikely now that any of this would ever be done, certainly, she had lost all enthusiasm for such matters. To her, the house and its patio were little more than a prison, from which he could foresee no escape.

She thought again of her parents. Did she dare ask

them for money to come home? They would hardly refuse. But the money would have to be borrowed from someone else. Or might she borrow the money herself? From Jeannie and Mark, perhaps? It seemed unlikely that their reserves would be that ample.

Her thoughts were interrupted by the opening and closing of a door. She turned her head to see Hank Blair descending the steps to his own patio.

She could not help but admire the magnificent physique, displayed so boldly in almost indecently brief swimming trunks. She experienced the same impression she had the first time she saw him. He was all man, the sort of man who could arouse excitement and desire in any woman. Even the aura of dissipation enhanced his sensual appeal.

His chest was broad, his waist and hips boyishly slender. There was no evidence of fat or softness to impair his masculinity. Laura had to admit to herself that, were she not married, she would find it difficult to resist a man so utterly physical.

He saw her and smiled, changing his course to walk toward her.

"Didn't know you were back from town," he said, towering over her.

"I just got here," she told him, trying to keep her eyes from his body and the all-too-obvious masculine appurtenances which the swim-trunks did little to conceal.

"Going down to the beach?" His eyes and the faint leer seemed to say that he knew exactly what she had been thinking.

She shrugged, trying to appear calm although she was growing rapidly ill at ease.

"I don't know—maybe a little later."

"We could stay around here a while," he suggested, the smile broadening. "Just the two of us. They'll be there for some time."

Laura blushed at the insinuation. She and Hank Blair, alone together. There was little doubt he would make advances.

She knew suddenly that such a situation would be totally disastrous. In her present state of mind she would not have the strength of character to resist the advances of this exciting, nearly-nude male.

She stood up abruptly, painfully aware of his closeness and of the currents racing between them.

"Maybe I will go to the beach after all," she said, moving quickly away from him toward the safety of her house. "I'll see you there in a few minutes."

She knew that he had not moved, that he was still standing there as she went into the kitchen. She could feel his eyes on her back as the door closed behind her.

She hurried into the bedroom, annoyed with herself. She had been actually aroused by the man. It was useless to kid herself about that. For a moment or two she had actually wanted to submit to him, to partake of the lustful pleasure he offered in such ample measure. Eve had given her physical release, but it was not the total rapture that only a man's body could provide a woman.

Even that thought was frightening. She had hoped to persuade Neil of the values to be found in substitution. But would such substitution ever compensate for the complete act? Judging from her reaction to Hank, it seemed unlikely.

I must get hold of myself, she thought.

She found her swim-suit in the dresser and laid it on the bed. As she undressed, she thought of Eve and Neil together on the beach.

"I'm probably the only woman in the world who doesn't have to worry because her husband is alone with Eve," she thought, bitterly amused by the reflection.

She put her sweater and skirt neatly away, bending to peel her hose from her shapely legs. She had only just straightened up when she heard a sound behind her. She whirled about to see Hank Blair framed in the doorway, smiling at her.

Laura blushed crimson, aware that she stood in nothing more than a skimpy bra and panties, and all too conscious of the gleam in his eyes.

"What are you doing here?" she demanded, aware that her voice sounded not so much angry as frightened. Her legs were trembling so that she wondered how long they would support her.

"Watching," he answered simply. "And enjoying the show immensely."

He moved from the doorway, coming slowly toward her, and the evidence of his arousal was like a shock to her.

"What do you want?" she whispered, unable to make herself move away from him.

He laughed aloud at that. "The same thing you want."

He was standing before her, so close that she could feel the heat of his body radiating out to her.

"You'll have to go." Her voice was small and sounded very far away even to her own ears.

His eyes held and caught hers. His hands, as he clasped her waist, seemed to sear her flesh.

"Do you want me to go?" He asked. "Try saying it aloud. Tell me, if you can, that you want me to leave."

Laura opened her mouth to say it, but the words stuck in her throat. She knew that she had to stop this before another second passed, yet she was powerless to break the spell that held her rooted to the spot.

He reached behind her, his large hands dealing efficiently with the clasp of her bra. It fell away, and her quivering breasts spilled into view.

His thumbs hooked in the elastic at her waist, peeling the white panties down over her hips. They fell about her feet. Like a puppet, moving at his bidding, she stepped free of the fabric.

She felt a surge of womanly pride as his eyes feasted on her naked charms, obviously pleased by what they saw. His strong arms pulled her toward him. Her breasts touched and were crushed by the rocklike firmness of his naked chest.

"We can't," she managed to whisper, but the rest of her protest was shut off by the demanding mouth that crushed her lips fiercely.

Her hands seemed to move of their own accord. With a shock she realized that she had hold of the waistband of his swimming trunks, was peeling them downward as he had done with her undergarments.

He was all that any woman could have desired, and then some. She knew that she had to have him, had to have the manly love his body promised. Nothing mattered in this moment but the hardness of him pinned against her yielding softness.

An eternity later, the kiss ended. He stepped back, swept her into his arms, carried her to the waiting bed in two long strides. Her heart pounded maddeningly as he threw himself upon her.

There was no softness or gentleness in him. His strong hands mauled her mercilessly, pawing savagely at the twin mountains of her breasts. His mouth tasted of each fiery peak, sending her into a crescendo.

"You really need it, don't you baby?" he whispered, laughing softly.

"Yes—*yes!*" she moaned.

She writhed in happy agony as his hands went to her moist thighs. She opened herself to him, welcoming him with a hunger that matched and surpassed his. With frantic hands she reached for him, guiding him eagerly to her, desperate for fulfillment.

She cried aloud at the swiftness of his entry. Her back arched, her hips thrust upward to welcome his attack. She met him thrust for thrust, panting as he surged violently upward, lifting her into a delirium of happiness.

His hands kneaded the tender softness of her buttocks. She could only cling to him, sobbing with joy as their tempo grew faster and faster. Their sweat-drenched bodies clung together furiously.

"I can't *stand* it!" she gasped, sobbing helplessly. "It's too wonderful!"

"Love me, baby!" he whispered hoarsely. His mouth found hers again, his tongue insistent and white-hot.

She felt as though she could endure no more, as though at any moment she would explode into a million pieces. Her body was a raging inferno that knew no control.

"Now!" she gasped. Her hands clawed at his naked back. She bit wildly into the flesh of his shoulder to stifle the scream that rose in her throat as torrents of passion swept through them, carrying them beyond time and space. His groans of ecstasy were loud in her ears and it was a long time before she realized that she, too, was crying aloud, *"This...is...it!"*

They drifted slowly back to earth, clinging weakly to one another as their ardor ebbed. She opened her eyes to see that satanic smile once more.

"Better than my wife?" he asked cruelly.

Laura blushed with shame and humiliation. She had given herself to him without resistance or protest, with the abandon of a savage animal. He had been vicious and primitive, and she had been all the more wanton for it.

He stood up, stretching contentedly, and donned the bathing suit that had been discarded an eternity before.

Laura stared for a moment at the naked beauty of his body. Then, ashamed, she turned her eyes away, trying to forget the wild pleasure his flesh had just afforded her.

He came back to the bed, crouching over her. She started to move away from him, but his rough hands pinned her to the spot, his mouth cruelly demanding subservience from hers. She hated herself for it, yet her body responded eagerly.

He laughed at her as he pulled abruptly away and stood again.

"You'd like it again, wouldn't you—right now?" he asked. "You're a hot one, all right. I don't know how you managed to say no the first time I asked."

Laura shuddered and closed her eyes. He was right, she would have been willing to submit to him again, that very moment. *What have I become?* she asked herself silently.

The floor creaked as he crossed the room. He was gone.

Dazed, Laura rose at last. Like a robot, she donned the bathing suit she had laid out earlier. She would have to face the others as though nothing had happened. To do otherwise would make the situation obvious. However bad things were between herself and Neil, she could not let him know to what lengths she had been driven. It would be cruel to let him know that another man had given her what he could not provide.

It can't happen again, she vowed silently as she left the house and started in the direction of the beach. She would never again allow herself to be alone with Eve or Hank Blair. She knew that it would happen again if she were ever alone with Hank Blair. No matter how much she hated herself for it, he had given her physical fulfillment beyond her wildest dreams. She would never be strong enough to refuse him.

She found the others lazily sprawled on blankets at the beach.

Hank was already there. He saw her first, and the smile that he flashed at her was so smug and self-satisfied as to have revealed the entire incident to everyone else had they been looking at him.

Laura saw Eve glance at her husband, then at her. Eve's expression made it plan that she knew the truth at once. She, too, smiled. Laura tried to ignore it. It scarcely mattered if Eve guessed. No doubt Hank would tell her about it later, anyway, sparing no details.

Neil did not see her approach until she dropped on the blanket beside him.

"Get everything taken care of?" he asked, innocent of all that his question implied.

Laura could not look at him as she answered softly, "Yes, I did."

She did not have to look at Eve or at Hank to know how Neil's remark must have amused them. They were laughing at her and at Neil.

In that moment, she hated them both. They had seen her and recognized her at once as a woman whose body was alive with desire. They had struck into her vulnerability to gratify their own lusts. As for herself, she had played into their hands at every turn. If they were evil, and immoral, then what was she?

CHAPTER TEN

Although it was a beautiful day for the beach, the four of them seemed unable to respond to anything other than their own thoughts. Hank Blair alone looked satisfied. Laura could not help but wonder how many women he had conquered. No doubt there had been many, for he was the sort to go after anything he wanted, and it was unlikely he had suffered many defeats.

Eve remained quiet and sullen. It was in a sense amusing that she seemed jealous of her husband's accomplishment, after all she had said to the contrary. *Perhaps,* Laura thought wryly, *she considered me her personal property.*

Laura herself remained withdrawn and unhappy, so much so that even Neil noticed it. He made one or two feeble attempts to cheer her, after which he, too, retired into lethargy.

After an hour, Laura gave up and decided to return to the house. She stood up, brushing sand from her legs.

"I guess I'm not in a sun-and-sand mood after all," she declared. "It's back to the house for me."

"I'll join you," Eve decided, standing also.

"Oh don't spoil your afternoon," Laura told her firmly. "I have a lot I want to get done."

She left without giving Eve a chance to put forth an argument. Let her sulk, she thought, striding across the sand toward the houses in the distance. She was in no mood for Eve's cynicism, and she regretted that Jeannie was gone. At least the pretty young wife was cheer-full and kind. She and her husband were the only ones in Sandy Knoll who appeared to have no ulterior motives in their friendships. The others were friendly or pleasant only for the sake of their own personal gains, mostly physical gains.

She saw Greta Hobbs in the distance. The other woman looked in her direction once, but neither of them waved or made any other gesture of recognition.

The house was cool and dark after the beach. Laura showered and changed clothes. The bed, she saw, was still rumpled. She smoothed it, trying not to remember Hank's masculine body over hers.

Neil came back a little later. His temporary rise in spirits had faded, and he was once again sullen and withdrawn. He showered and dressed again, after which he headed straight for the bar.

"You don't care much for Eve Blair, do you?" he asked, peering over the rim of his glass at Laura.

Laura shrugged, wondering how she could prevent the conversation from becoming another nasty argument.

"She's all right," she answered finally.

"Maybe you're jealous of her." Neil continued to

study her intently.

Laura's heart stopped for an instant. "Jealous of her? Why should I be?"

"You might be hot for that husband of hers. He's quite a man. I'll bet most women would like a toss in the hay with him."

Laura turned her back on him deliberately, although she was far less calm than she appeared. Did he suspect the truth about her and Hank, or was he only searching for something to argue about? He might have caught the glances and remarks at the beach, and guessed their significance. It was even possible that Eve Blair had said something to him for the sheer sake of causing trouble.

"I don't like your insinuation," she told him curtly, hoping that her indignation sounded genuine.

"What would you do if he asked you to go to bed with him?" Neil pursued.

"I'd slap his face," Laura answered quickly.

She left the room, without giving him an opportunity to pursue the subject further, and began to wash the dishes in the sink.

Neil left the subject where it was. Instead, he devoted all his attention to getting drunk. He seemed completely oblivious to her presence in the house as the day went on. Eager to avoid argument, Laura left him alone, remaining in the kitchen as much as possible.

It was nearly evening when he came into the kitchen. She was preparing dinner. He came directly to her, taking her roughly in his arms.

She knew what was coming. He was going to try again. He reached for the swell of her breasts beneath her blouse. The liquor on his breath was harsh and unpleasant in her nostrils.

"Stop it!" she ordered sharply, moving away from him.

"Who the hell do you think you are?" he demanded angrily, starting for her again. "I'm your husband. Have you forgotten that? Or would you prefer that I was Hank? I'll bet you wouldn't pull away from *him* like that."

"Leave me alone!" she shouted. "I don't want another quarrel!"

He stopped, staring coldly at her.

"I mean it, Neil," she went on, determined that the incidents of the past would not repeat themselves this time. "If you try to force me, I swear I'll have our marriage annulled, regardless of how much it embarrasses you."

The look he gave her held pure hatred but the threat had its desired effect. After a moment of silence, he turned sharply and went out the door. She heard the roar of the car in the drive, then he drove wildly away.

Laura stood shaken and alone in the kitchen. Where was it all leading? What would happen to them? Surely they couldn't go on like this. With each passing moment she became more confused, more uncertain of what to do about things. She could no longer think clearly.

She decided that she needed a drink. Abandoning the dinner, she mixed herself a martini. She had just settled on the sofa with it when there was a knock at the back door, and Eve called to her.

Without inviting her to come in, Laura hurried to the back door, grateful that she had remembered earlier to latch it.

"Any plans for the evening?" Eve asked. She did not comment on the latched door, although Laura had no doubts that she had noticed it.

"I don't know," Laura replied. "Neil went out."

"That's too bad." Eve smiled as if to indicate she had heard the argument and already knew that Neal was out. It was, Laura reminded herself, quite possible.

"I told Jeannie I'd look after Mark," Eve was saying. "He's the helpless type. He's going to come over for a bite with us this evening. I thought maybe you'd like to join us."

"I already have dinner started," Laura said. Impulsively, she added, "But I could stop over afterward."

Surely, she told herself, there could be no harm in that. Hank and Eve would be there, and Mark as well. Nothing could happen.

"Fine," Eve agreed. "See you later, then."

When she was gone, Laura wondered about the wisdom of accepting the invitation. Neither Eve nor Hank offered much protection from the advances of the other.

It was Mark's company, however, that finally calmed her doubts. He was hardly the sort to go along with any dirty schemes they might have....

Laura did not eat her dinner after all. She sat at the table, picking at her food for a long time, but she had no appetite. Neil had not returned, nor could she honestly regret his absence. It was too much of an ordeal, avoiding arguments when he was around.

Giving up on the meal, she changed into a fresh skirt and blouse, threw a sweater over her shoulders and crossed the patios to the Blair house.

"Hi, you're just in time," Eve greeted her at the door.

"For what?" Laura asked, apprehensive. Maybe after all she had misjudged Mark.

"For a drink, silly. We just finished dinner."

Eve led the way into the living room, where the men were seated. Greeting Mark, Laura was impressed again with his clean-cut, youthful charm. She could not help thinking how perfect he was for Jeannie and how happy they must be together. Her doubts were assuaged again by his presence.

"Scotch?" Hank asked from the bar. Laura hesitated for a moment. She was not much of a drinker, and the martini had already left her a little lightheaded. Her resistance, however, was too low to refuse. She nodded.

"I just suggested to Mark that we see some movies," Hank said when he handed her the large drink. "We've got some pretty good ones."

"Fine," Laura answered, seating herself on the sofa beside Mark, although at a discreet distance. She was puzzled by the surprised look he gave her, but he looked away quickly and she had no opportunity to question him.

"Good idea," Eve agreed cheerfully. She left the room and came back in a minute with a portable screen, which she set up near one wall. Hank wheeled in a projector, and in a few minutes they were sitting in the dark, staring at the glaring light on the screen.

The film started with a shot of an ordinary-looking bedroom. A woman entered the room. Laura was suddenly suspicious. She had assumed they were going to see home movies, perhaps vacation films. Now she understood the surprised look Mark had given her when she had agreed to the suggestion. She had heard of movies prepared for men—at least she had always thought of them that way. It seemed that these movies were of that sort.

Her suspicions were confirmed when the woman on the screen lifted her arms and began to remove her sweater, pulling it slowly over her head. She had nothing under it and her huge, rather flabby, breasts swung indolently to and fro on the screen.

Laura sat stiffly, wishing there were some way to escape from the room, knowing that she could not do so without looking foolish. She drank the scotch-and-water nervously and altogether too rapidly.

The woman on the screen was by now completely nude. She posed for a few minutes, turning to show every possible view of her. Then, to Laura's amazement, she was joined by another woman. This one was already naked. The two embraced and moved to the bed.

Laura stared in horrified fascination as the two began an act of sexual interplay, for all the world as though they were truly alone and not being watched by the eye of the camera.

She had never seen anything of this sort. Even when she had enjoyed Eve's embraces, it had been in darkness. The thought of being watched during such an act was repulsive to her. Even witnessing the scene enacted on the screen was unpleasant, yet she felt her urges stirring within her as she watched the two women build to a feverish climax. It was as though she were sharing the experience with them.

She had assumed the movie would end when they had finished, but she was again mistaken. The two women remained on the bed, and in another moment still another participant appeared on the screen, a naked young man.

The man was, Laura guessed, not more than eighteen or nineteen and quite attractive. He was the type one sees in magazine ads, clean-cut and fresh. But his expression was one of lustful anticipation and it was plain that he was ready for action.

As Laura watched him join the two women, she had to admit that the sight was intensely stimulating. She could not watch the show without remembering Hank and his passionate demands upon her.

She was weak with disgust and at the same time filled with aroused desire when it finally ended. The light came on abruptly, and Eve moved to refill their glasses.

Laura blinked her eyes and tried to conceal her embarrassment. She glanced in Mark's direction, and saw instantly that he, also, had been aroused by the movie. She felt sympathy for him, however, as she saw that he, too, was quite embarrassed.

"More?" Hank asked.

Laura looked up to see that he was staring directly at her. His smile seemed to be daring her.

"I think we could all use a breather," she told him in an even voice. She would not give him the satisfaction of knowing that he had upset her.

"Anyway," Eve said, dropping into an easy chair, "those things get tedious after a while. Personally, I prefer the real thing."

"Now there's a good suggestion," Hank agreed. He regarded the two on the sofa. "Anyone interested?"

Laura looked quickly away from him, relieved to see that Mark was blushing also.

"I don't think so," she said aloud, although her voice was less even this time.

"What a pair of duds," Eve sneered. "Maybe we could give them a real show." She addressed the latter remarks to her husband.

Hank shrugged, grinned also. Laura had the impression that they had planned all this to taunt her and, perhaps, Mark as well. After all, it was more than likely that Eve had her eyes on Mark. No doubt they thought this would put him in the mood.

"Tell you what," Hank said, standing and beginning at once to remove his shirt. "We'll start and see if you two don't change your minds."

They did not wait for their guests' permission, confident there would be no objection. As Laura and Mark watched from the sofa, husband and wife stripped with speed and a conspicuous lack of modesty.

They were, Laura had to admit, a handsome pair. It was difficult for her to see Hank's magnificent naked body without feeling desire for him again, yet she could not tear her eyes from the two.

They embraced, brazenly toying with one another. Eve led the way to the other sofa across the room, lowering herself to it. Hank hovered over her, bringing himself slowly down toward her.

Laura found it impossible to believe that they were actually performing the act there, in the light, for her and Mark to see. Had they no shame at all, no scruples?

"Anyone want to join us?" Eve called from the sofa.

"I don't think so," Mark said curtly. He stood and, to Laura's amazement, he reached and took her arm.

"Come on," he said tersely. "I think it's time we both left."

She went with him gladly, little caring what the Blairs might think. The fresh cool air of the patio was a welcome relief. They stood together in the darkness, both of them trembling slightly. Laura looked up into the gentle softness of his eyes, trying to smile.

"'I suspect that was staged for our benefit," he said nervously.

"I thought so myself."

"I'll be honest. Another minute and I wouldn't have

been able to get up and walk out."

They stared into one another's eyes for a moment. Then he pulled her quickly to him, his arms tight about her.

It was a very sudden and very brief kiss. There was scarcely time for her to react before he let her go and stepped back.

"I'm sorry," he apologized, looking so sheepish that she almost threw her arms about him to comfort him. "That sort of thing is disgusting, but the worst of it is, it *is* stimulating. You can't help but be excited by it."

"I know what you mean," she told him, touching his shoulder gently and affectionately. "I'm glad you dragged me out of there when you did."

He stared down at her for a moment longer, with an expression she couldn't decipher.

"Let's walk," he suggested.

Grateful for his company, Laura slipped her arm through his, and the two of them made their way slowly through the darkness toward the distant murmur of the ocean.

She thought of the scene Eve and Hank had enacted for them and of what Mark had said. It had been stimulating—frightfully so. Another moment, and both of them would have been too far gone to say no. Even now, her body was warm with aroused ardor, and she was painfully aware of the nearness of Mark, and of his attractiveness.

With a shiver, she thrust that thought from her mind.

CHAPTER ELEVEN

The moon had risen, casting its silver light over the dark water. Laura leaned close to Mark as they walked, grateful for the protective warmth of his arm. She thought again of Jeannie, of how fortunate Jeannie was. She herself would have given virtually anything to have a husband like Mark.

They reached the water and stopped, staring out into the vast distance. It was a romantic setting. Laura felt not even the slightest fear as Mark turned her face gently toward his, and once again kissed her, this time less quickly.

He was again apologetic, however, when they separated.

"What I need is to cool off," he said with a nervous laugh. "How about a swim?"

"I'd love to," Laura agreed. Then her face fell. "Oh, dear, if we go back for our suits, they'll be sure to see us and spoil everything by wanting to come along. I don't think I could take any more of Eve and Hank tonight."

"All right, we'll go without suits." He grinned playfully as he made the suggestion, challenging her.

She laughed in return. "All right," she agreed.

At another time, she might have been shocked by his suggestion, just as at another time he would probably not have made it. But the stimulation of the raunchy films to which they had been exposed earlier, the strong drinks and the mood of this moment had put modesty out of their minds.

Laura stripped rapidly, her back to Mark. She stacked her clothes neatly in the soft grass that grew beyond the edge of the sand. When she had finished, she turned in Mark's direction.

He was just removing his socks. She could not help but think how different he was in every way from Neil, and from Hank Blair. Mark seemed much younger than either of them, although she knew for a fact that he must be very nearly the same age as Neil.

He was smaller as well, slender in a boyish, taut way. His skin glowed with youthful radiance. He looked up and saw her standing before him, naked in the silvery moonlight.

"Wow!" He whistled softly in appreciation of her loveliness.

Laura blushed, but she did not turn or move away. She was pleased by his honest admiration, and she could almost feel his gaze as he took in the lovely curves of her body. His eyes lingered on the pink tipped mounds of her breasts, and then glided downward to the whiteness of her thighs, adorned now with shadows.

"Come on," he exclaimed, grabbing her hand playfully. "We'd better get into that water, before I forget myself altogether."

They ran lightly and spiritedly across the sand, flinging themselves together into the sparkling surf. The water was cold, and its first touch upon their feet and ankles was shocking. Laura gasped and would have stopped, but Mark held tightly to her hand, pulling her along with him. They plunged deeper into the water with a giant whooshing sound.

It was delightful. They swam happily together, diving and splashing about. They played tag and ducked one another. Finally, out of breath, they raced back to the beach like two little children, scrambling across the sand to collapse in the cool grass near their clothes.

"I'm pooped!" Laura declared.

Mark went to where his clothes were and came back in a minute with his undershirt in his hands. Without a word, he began to rub her dry.

She sat contentedly as his hands efficiently restored the warmth to her body. She wished there were some way she could express her gratitude to him. This was the happiest she had been since her marriage, and she could not help but feel drawn to this pleasant young man beside her.

He finished drying her back. "Okay, the other side," he directed.

As Laura moved to turn toward him, his hand accidentally touched one swaying breast.

The contact was electrifying, awakening them both at once to the realization that they were man and woman, alone and naked in the darkness. They sat frozen for a moment, looking deeply into one another's eyes. Mark's hand came slowly back to the breast, caressing and fondling flesh with timid, hesitant movements.

Laura's arms lifted slowly, encircling his neck. He bent toward her and kissed her for the third time.

The affection between them grew slowly into something warmer, something more hungry and demanding. His hands kneaded her breasts with gradually increasing intensity. Then, slowly, tenderly, he pressed her into the grass.

Laura lay with her eyes closed, her bosom heaving, as his gently persuasive mouth traced its way over her body, arousing her progressively to more and more ardent plateaus. He kissed her warm thighs, his tongue igniting the moistness there.

Back up past her stomach, to the cherry red nipples, nibbling insistently, finally, his mouth returned to hers, his arms holding her close. She caressed his body unashamedly, enjoying the lean hardness of it, the satin smoothness of his skin, the rippling play of wiry muscles beneath the skin.

He fondled her body unceasingly, with ever increasing urgency. Their desire for one another rose more and more. His hand stroked the satin verge of her thighs, pleading for a welcome.

"Yes," she whispered, parting her legs to him. "Take me, Mark, please take me."

"You're sure?" he asked in a whisper. "We shouldn't—I shouldn't let you."

"It doesn't matter," she assured him. So much had happened, wrong and evil, but for this she would have no regrets.

He lowered himself to her, his ardor overcoming his hesitancy. She welcomed the lean, slender hips between her thighs, thrilled at the demanding hardness of his touch.

He was altogether different from Hank Blair. There was no cruelty, no vicious ravishing of her loveliness. He was eager to give as well as to receive, determined she should enjoy and be made complete in their union.

She rose willingly, happily, to the thrust of his taut hips. It was not an act of desperation, but of joy, of tenderness and beauty. Her cries as their locked bodies pitched and thrust were not cries of frustration but of delight. He answered her with soft, breathless moans of pleasure.

"You're so wonderful," he whispered.

His hands stroked her body lovingly all the while, as though unable to get enough of the soft warmth of her flesh. Naked skin buffeted against naked skin, pulse throbbed with pulse, as they ascended toward a heaven of mutual ecstasy.

Their passion became a tempest that swept away everything ugly and unpleasant. Her legs locked about him, urging him into her very depths, and he went hungrily, happily. The thudding of body against body blended with the rush of the surf, their flesh gleamed in the silver whiteness of the moonlight.

"Yes, *yes!*" she groaned aloud, writhing and

thrashing beneath him.

Wildly they rocked and heaved, lost in a rapture of physical joy.

Laura stiffened and jerked, and suddenly burst and exploded in a shower of stars. Mark crushed her to him, riding out the storm of her fulfillment and then, in a wild frenzy of motion, he rushed after her, releasing himself at last with deep groans of delight.

They lay locked together, too awed by what had happened between them to speak or to stir. Time stood still as they savored the lingering sweetness of perfect union.

"It was beautiful," she was able to say at last, stroking his tousled hair affectionately.

He lifted his face to look down at her.

"I've never done this before," he told her honestly. "Cheating on Jeannie, I mean. But I can't say I'm sorry about it. I'll never forget this night."

The mood of tender affection was shattered suddenly. Neil's voice boomed angrily across the emptiness of the beach.

"That's what I call a pretty picture," he shouted. "Eve knew what she was talking about when she told me where to find the two of you."

They looked up to see him standing only a few feet away. There was little doubt that he had seen them, nor could there possibly be any doubt that he knew what they had been doing.

They jumped apart, Mark trying to scramble to his feet. But Neil, despite his evident drunkenness, was too quick. The toe of his shoe caught Mark viciously in the side, sending him sliding across the sand.

Laura cried aloud in fright, more for Mark than for herself. What had happened was as much her fault as his, perhaps more.

"Don't!" she cried as Neil raised his foot to kick again.

He stared at her with a look of loathing and violent anger. Then, with a loud oath, he whirled about and dashed back toward the house. Laura half rose to run after him but instead went to Mark who was sitting holding his side.

"I guess I had that coming," he said, forcing a smile.

"Don't say that," she pleaded impulsively, holding his head to her breasts. "It was too wonderful for us to regret it now."

"Maybe you'd better not go home now," he said, his concern touchingly obvious. "Give him a chance to sleep it off."

"I'll be all right," she assured him, although far from confident herself. "Chances are he'll have passed out by the time I get there anyway."

They dressed quickly and without conversation. Then Mark took her arm and they walked together toward the lights of the houses. When they reached the patio, however, Mark steered her firmly away from her house.

"At least come have some coffee, anyway, and give him a chance to cool off a little."

Laura did not argue. She went with him, noticing as

they passed that the Blairs were still up.

"Wonder if they're still at it?" he said as they went past.

"They must have paused long enough to send Neil after us," she reminded him. "But by now they may have lured some people in from the highway."

They laughed together, and entered Mark's house, taking time to close the curtains at the windows before flicking on the lights.

Mark made the coffee. They drank it leisurely, not saying much to one another.

Laura was right. By the time she arrived home, Neil had passed out. He was sprawled across the sofa, still clothed, dead to the world. Laura left him where he was and went to bed. For the first time in days, she slept deeply and without dreams.

CHAPTER TWELVE

Laura awoke with a smile on her face. The smile broadened as she thought of Mark Lane and what they had shared on the beach the previous night. That was how it should be for a man and a woman. She was certain that neither Neil nor Hank, both of whom gave the impression of being more virile than Mark, would ever be able to give the joy that he could give a woman.

Her smile faded as she thought of Neil, remembering the hideous conclusion of the scene on the beach. There was no longer anything to hide from Neil, no way to spare his feelings. The time had unquestionably come for her to make some decisions regarding her marriage to Neil.

It had been a mistake from the first and could only become worse. Already there had been Eve and Hank, who had satisfied her sexual desires, and finally Mark. Without a doubt there would ultimately be others willing and able to fulfill a husband's obligations. It was better to end things with Neil now than to allow the situation to go on as it was.

Assuredly, Neil would be hurt by having the marriage annulled. But there was no longer any justification for trying to spare Neil's feelings by continuing with the farce of their marriage. It would be far kinder of her to be cruel now.

She got up from the bed and tiptoed to the door to find her husband still asleep on the sofa. She made her way to the bathroom as quietly as possible and showered.

Neil was still on the sofa when she returned to the living room dressed for the day. He opened one eye and glared at her.

"Off to see your boyfriend?" he asked, sitting up unsteadily.

"No, as a matter of fact I was just on my way to make some coffee," she answered him calmly. She no longer feared Neil nor his moods.

"That was quite a show last night," he persisted, following her in to the kitchen. "How long have you two been sneaking around together?"

He was, she knew, being deliberately cruel.

"It just happened last night," she explained, knowing even as she spoke that it would be futile. His mood would not be so easily dispelled. "We didn't plan it, it just happened."

"Bitch!" He struck out suddenly, slapping her violently across the face. Laura staggered backward, bumping into the range.

"How many others have there been? You've been sleeping with the whole damn bunch of them, haven't you?"

"Yes!" she shouted back at him. "Yes, it wasn't only

Mark. There was Eve Blair as well, and her husband. Yes, Hank Blair made love to me too—right here in our house, on our bed!"

He grabbed her arm in a vise like grip. "I could kill you for this! Why did you do it?"

"Because I'm a woman, a woman with needs and desires like any other woman, and you...." She stopped without finishing the sentence.

"...And I'm not a man." He finished it for her. "That's what you were going to say, isn't it? Well, I'll prove to you that you're wrong. I'll prove that I'm a man, damn you!"

She thought he would hit her again, but she was saved by a voice that came from the back door—Mark's voice.

"It wasn't only her fault," he said calmly but firmly. "If you want to take it out on someone, why not make it me instead?"

Without waiting to be answered, he stepped into the kitchen. Laura held her breath, not knowing what to expect from Neil.

"I've come to apologize," Mark went on. "I know it won't do much good, but I owe you that much at least."

"Go to hell!" Neil shouted at him.

To Laura's relief, Neil whirled about and charged out of the room. The front door crashed after him, and a minute later the car roared out of the drive with a squeal of tires.

Laura and Mark stood facing one another across the kitchen. He managed to smile a tired, embarrassed smile.

"I owe you an apology too."

She shook her head vigorously. "No, I owe you my thanks. I know what I have to do now, and I've made up my mind to do it. As for last night, this may sound shameless of me, but I loved it."

"So did I," he admitted softly. He sighed and looked away from her. "Jeannie's coming back this morning. I don't know how I can face her."

Laura reached for him tenderly." Let me tell her," she offered. "I'll meet her bus, and I'll tell her on the way home. I owe her that much."

"That sounds like the easy way out for me. I hate being a coward."

"No, it isn't that at all, Mark. There's a great deal that you don't know—about me, about the Blairs. She should know all of it. I think it will help her to understand what happened, and why."

He nodded finally. "Okay, if that's what you want. Take my car when you go. I'll catch cab into town and kill some time there."

He pulled his car keys from his pocket and dropped them lightly on the table. Then, impulsively, he caught her in his arms, pulling her quickly to him. His lips found hers in a long, moving kiss.

They both knew that with Jeannie's return there could never be anything between them again. But this was here and now, and they were in one another's arms. The memory of the night before replenished the ardor of their vital young bodies.

"I'd like to," she told him softly.

"So would I," he answered. They walked slowly, hand in hand, into the bedroom.

"Neil?"

"He won't be home," Laura assured him. "And if he comes in, he won't see anything more than he saw last night."

Mark undressed her gently, without haste, pausing as each piece of clothing fell away, his eyes and his hands caressing each portion of her body as it was revealed to him.

When she was naked, she helped him to undress also. She had never before felt such desire to examine and search a man's body. She thrilled at the sight and feel of him, shamelessly scrutinizing his nakedness. She was impressed anew by his youth, and yet he was plainly a man, his eager body giving large evidence of his desire for her.

He took her hand and led her to the bed. There was no haste, no driving need. His mouth, gently eager, examined all of her, fueling the fire of her passion. She in turn tasted of his body, exploring him with her mouth as she had with her eyes and hands.

When at last he came to her, her thighs opened warmly to him, and once again their bodies were joined together in the ritual of love....

It seemed an eternity later that he rose from the bed. Laura watched him dress, intoxicated with the sight of his strong young body as he moved.

She could not regret having given herself to him,

especially since she knew that this had been their last time together. There would be a Mark of her own somewhere, a young man who would give her happiness, love and pleasure, and to whom she could give as much.

He came back to stand over her for a moment.

"Thank you," he said simply. Then he bent and kissed her quickly before leaving.

When he was gone, Laura rose from the bed and dressed slowly. She found herself regretting that she had not met Mark before he had met Jeannie, before she had married Neil. *No, that's wrong,* she told herself emphatically. *Jeannie is a wonderful girl, and she deserves a wonderful guy like Mark.*

It was wrong to wish for someone else's husband. In time, she would find one of her own, the right one.

The keys to Mark's car were still on the table in the kitchen. With them was a brief note from Mark that said simply *The twelve o'clock bus.*

Laura crumpled up the note and threw it away. Her watch told her it was eleven o'clock. In another hour she would meet Jeannie, and would have to tell her the truth—that she and Mark had been to bed together; that they had made love to one another. No doubt Jeannie would hate her for it, but it was time to be honest.

Deliberately, she climbed into Mark's car, started up the motor and headed for Santa Monica.

She arrived at the bus terminal well ahead of time. As she waited, she smoked several cigarettes, pacing back and forth across the small waiting room.

There was much that she would have to do, once she delivered Jeannie home and told her the truth about herself and Mark. First, she would have to talk to Neil, drunk or sober. It would be simpler just to leave, but she felt that she owed it to him to tell him in advance that she was going to have their marriage annulled.

She had enough money of her own left to take an inexpensive room somewhere. After that, she would have to find herself some sort of job. It would not be easy, but the easy way is not always the best.

She regretted the necessity for hurting Neil further, just as she regretted having already hurt him. In time, perhaps, he could forgive her, but for now they could only hope to destroy one another by going on together.

The bus arrived after an eternity of waiting. Laura dropped her cigarette, grinding it out nervously with the heel of her shoe, and looked for Jeannie among the passengers leaving the vehicle. She saw her finally, looking incredibly young and innocent, and waved to her. Jeannie waved back, and came toward her with a puzzled smiled on her face.

"Where's Mark?" she asked, falling into step beside Laura.

"He was tied up," Laura explained lamely. "I said I would pick you up."

"That was sweet of you, but I could have taken a cab home easily enough."

"I wanted to do it," Laura told her.

They were at the car now. Laura slid into the driver's seat, waiting for Jeannie to take her place in the car also before saying more.

"I wanted a chance to talk to you."

Jeannie gave her a curious glance, but said nothing, waiting for Laura to explain in her own way.

Laura started the car and steered into the flow of traffic heading towards Sandy Knoll. "Is anything wrong?" Jeannie asked at last.

"Yes," Laura answered. Then, seeing Jeannie's frightened expression, she added quickly "Oh, Mark's all right, it's nothing like that. It's just that—well, something happened while you were gone. Mark and I.... *Damn!* I don't know how to say it."

"You made love?" Jeannie put it into words for her.

Laura nodded her head. "Yes. I wanted to be the one to tell you about it, to try to explain it to you. We were at Eve and Hank's. There were drinks, and they showed movies. Do you know the kind of movies they show?"

"Eve described them to me." Jeannie was staring straight ahead of the car, her face perfectly blank. "I've never seen them."

"They're pretty raw. Afterward, they put on a little show of their own for our benefit. Then Mark and I left. We went down to the beach together. Neither one of us intended anything to happen, but we were more aroused than we realized."

There were several long minutes of silence between them. Laura wondered if Jeannie expected her to say something more, but she could think of nothing further to say.

"I can understand," Jeannie said finally. "I know about Neil—Eve told me that. It must have been very difficult for you."

"Can you forgive me?" If she were in Jeannie's shoes, Laura wondered, could she be forgiving?

"I don't know," Jeannie admitted bluntly. "I'd like to hate you for it, but I don't think I can. Is this why Mark didn't come for me?"

"He was sorry, and ashamed. I asked him to let me. Please try to forgive him. He loves you terribly."

Jeannie said nothing more. They drove on in silence. Arriving finally at Sandy Knoll, Laura turned into the gates and on down the street that led to her house. Jeannie's house was first. She turned into the drive and switched off the engine.

"I'll walk over from here," she said, climbing out of the car and starting toward her own house.

"Laura," Jeannie called after her.

Laura paused, looking back over her shoulder.

"Don't hate yourself too much."

Laura smiled gratefully before going on. She wondered if Mark were home, and if it would be difficult for Jeannie to forgive him. Would this mar the happiness of their marriage permanently? Surely not—they were so plainly in love, so obviously right for one another, and Jeannie was intelligent enough to realize that.

She saw the car in their driveway, and knew that Neil was home again. *If only he's sober,* she thought, but without much hope he would be.

She would have to tell him even at the risk of violence. She could not spend another night in that house. She had fallen as low as she intended to go.

"Don't hate yourself too much...." Jeannie had said after Laura had betrayed her. Somehow she must bring Jeannie to trust her again, and respect her. But first she would have to learn once more to trust and respect herself, something she had ceased doing.

Neil was plainly drunk and as clearly determined to be ugly. He glared viciously at her as she let herself into the house.

"You've been out with your boy friend, haven't you?" he demanded.

Laura stopped in the center of the room, determined not to be intimidated.

"No, I haven't," she answered him calmly. "I picked up Jeannie at the station, and brought her home."

Neil's eyes narrowed. "His wife? What if I told her about it?"

"She already knows. *I* told her."

"Maybe you did and maybe you didn't."

Laura sighed wearily. "I don't want to argue with you Neil, and I don't want any more unhappiness for either of us. I just want to tell you that it won't work for us. It can't work, not now or ever. I think we both know that by this time. I'm going to leave you, today. Monday, I'll see about having the marriage annulled."

"You can't do that," he shouted drunkenly.

"I can, and I will," she insisted. "Any doctor will testify that you would never consummate the marriage.

It will be difficult for you, I know, and I'm truly sorry, but we can't go on."

He snarled and threw his drink across the room. The glass shattered with a crash against the wall.

"You think I'm not a man," he roared, shaking his fist at her. "But I am. I told you it almost happened the last time...."

She shook her head firmly. "It was an illusion, Neil, nothing happened. You only imagined it."

"That's a lie!" He came toward her as though to hit her, but he stopped shortly in front of her. "It's a lie, I'll prove it to you!"

Laura shuddered in the face of his anger. She was fearful of his statement, of what he might do to try to prove what he said.

"Neil, please...!" she tried to reason with him.

He spat at her and whirled about, storming out the back door.

Weakly, Laura dropped on to the sofa, holding her head in her hands. She had done what she could. There was nothing more for her to do but gather together a few of her things and leave. She could get the rest some other time when she knew that Neil was out. She had no wish to see him again.

It took only a short while to pack some of her clothes into a suitcase. She set it down by the front door and started to telephone for a cab.

"I'll say good-bye to Jeannie," she decided, pausing at the phone, "and ask her if I can call her when I get settled somewhere."

She left her suitcase where it was, and went the back way to Jeannie's house. The Blairs, she was happy to notice, were apparently away from home. She had no desire to say goodbye to either of them.

There was no answer to her knock at Jeannie's door. Laura stood at the steps and gazed questioningly at the window. She knew Jeannie was home, or at least she had delivered her there a short while before. She went around to the front of the house. Yes, the car was still in the drive, exactly where she had left it.

She went around to the back again, making her way in the direction of the beach. There was no one as far as she could see in either direction.

Laura returned to her own house, more depressed than before. Jeannie had plainly not gone out. She must have seen Laura approach the house, and had deliberately ignored the knock at her door.

"I can't blame her for not wanting to see me," Laura admitted glumly to herself, but there was little consolation in the admission.

She went through the house once more, going to the telephone in the living room again to call a cab. As she dialed, her eyes went about the room, taking it all in for the last time. She looked through the window, and saw the blue fender of Neil's car in the drive.

Neil's car? But of course, he had gone out the back door, and she had not heard him drive away. But where on earth had he gone? He had not been on the beach, she had not seen him outside.

Her heart seemed to stop beating as the answer

began to dawn on her. He had not believed her when she had told him that Jeannie knew the truth about the night before. He might very well have gone over there himself to tell her...but no, she had been there, and Jeannie hadn't answered the door...what was it that Neil had been shouting at her? That he would prove himself a man.

Laura thought of Jeannie, alone in her house, and of Neil in his drunken rage. His wife had been unfaithful to him, with another man. What better way to take his revenge than with the other man's wife?

CHAPTER THIRTEEN

Laura ran out of her house and down the street toward Jeannie's She ran up to the front door and pounded loudly, calling Jeannie's name. There was no answer. More frightened with each passing minute, she tried the door. It was locked.

She ran around the house, to the back door. It was locked also. She stood and stared at the door, feeling maddeningly helpless. She could not possibly force the door, not by herself. The Blairs were out somewhere. There was no telling when they would return.

Did she dare call the police? There was still the possibility that Neil was not inside, that Jeannie was only ignoring her. It would all look pretty silly if she had to explain that to the police.

She walked slowly around the house again, trying to think of something reasonable to do. As she reached the front, a taxicab pulled up at the curb, and she saw Mark get out. She ran to meet him as he started up the walk.

"Hi," he greeted her, puzzled by her appearance. "What's happening?"

"Mark, it's Neil," she told him breathlessly, almost

afraid to admit what she was thinking. "He left the house drunk and in a pretty ugly mood, he said he was going to prove that he was a man. When I came over here later to say goodbye to Jeannie, the door was locked and there was no answer. I was worried...."

Mark didn't wait for her to finish explaining. He was past her and up the steps in three fast strides. By the time Laura had reached the door, he had unlocked it and was inside.

She ran after him. He headed straight for the bedroom.

Her fears had been correct. Neil was there, with Jeannie. Laura froze in the doorway, staring in horror.

Jeannie's clothes were strewn about the room where they had fallen as Neil had ripped them off of her. Jeannie herself lay sprawled across the bed, a stocking binding her hands together and holding them to the headboard. Another stocking held a gag in place across her mouth.

Neil was crouched over her on the bed, nearly as naked as she. His back was to the door, and as they entered the room, he raised his fist and struck Jeannie cruelly in the mouth.

"You son of a bitch!" Mark roared. He charged across the room, so suddenly that Neil scarcely had time to realize what was happening. The two of them tumbled to the floor beside the bed, toppling night-stands and lamps as they fell.

Laura stood petrified, watching the two of them grappling with one another. Neil had the advantage of size and bull-like strength. But in his favor, Mark was sober and was fighting with the anger of a protective bear. Laura knew that he would kill Neil if he were able. Nor did she doubt for a moment that Neil would do the same if things went his way.

Neil managed to get on top of his opponent, pinning Mark to the floor. Here his size and sheer weight served him well. Mark struggled to free himself from the crushing grip.

For a moment or so, Laura thought the fight was ended. Then, with a superhuman burst of power, Mark broke free from his opponent. He stumbled away, but Neil went after him, landing a blow that sent Mark crashing into the wall.

How long would Mark be able to endure? Laura asked herself. He was already badly battered, while Neil was just warming up. Blood spurted from Mark's mouth as Neil's fist landed again. Mark's legs crumpled. He fell to his knees only to catch the point of Neil's shoe beneath his chin.

Mark went down all the way. Unexpectedly, however, he took Neil with him, grasping at the thick knees as he fell. Neil swayed, off balance, and crashed heavily to the floor. His head thudded soundly against the edge of the dresser, leaving him almost unconscious. It was his turn now to reel. Scarcely able to lift himself to his knees, Mark swung again and again, raining blows upon Neil, who seemed almost unaware of what was happening.

Laura moved quickly aside as Neil rose stumbled,

turned, and came in her direction. He staggered past her, out the door and out of the house. With a muttered oath, Mark started after him.

"Let him go," Laura told him, grabbing his arm. "Help me with Jeannie."

That had the intended effect. He helped awkwardly as Laura untied Jeannie's hands and removed the cloth from her mouth. Jeannie sobbed hysterically as she fell into her husband's arms.

"Oh Mark, it was awful. He tried...."

"It's okay, don't talk about it," he told her, stroking her naked body reassuringly.

"But he couldn't," she sobbed, turning her tear filled eyes up to him. "He tried, but he couldn't. And he became more violent than ever. He beat me, he said it was my fault, and he would kill me if it didn't work."

Laura could scarcely bear to hear about it. In a sense, it was her fault. At the very least, she should have realized that Neil might try something of this sort. Jeannie again had paid the price for Laura's folly.

Jeannie collapsed into her husband's arms. Laura found a robe in the closet and brought it to the bed, slipping it gently about Jeannie's shoulders.

"Stay with her," Mark said, steering his wife tenderly but firmly into Laura's arms.

"Mark, where are you going?" Laura asked, frightened by the wild anger still evident in his eyes.

"I'm not finished with him yet," he shouted as he went out of the room.

"Oh, stop him," Jeannie pleaded, struggling to free

herself from Laura's grip. "Neil's insane, he'll kill Mark."

"I'll try," Laura told her, starting to get up. "If you'll stay here."

"No!" Jeannie grabbed her arm frantically, her eyes wide with terror. "No, don't leave me here alone—please! He might come back."

Laura hesitated uncertainly. Jeannie was beyond reason at the moment; it would be cruel to leave her alone in her present state of mind. Yet she was frightened for Mark. Neil was out of his mind. There was no telling what he might do.

"Come with me," Laura decided. She helped Jeannie to her feet and the two of them walked unsteadily to the front of the house.

From the sidewalk out front, Neil and Mark were plainly visible. They were on the lawn outside Neil's house, tossing and tumbling about on the grass. The two women watched in helpless fear as the fight continued.

Jeannie gasped suddenly in alarm. Laura stiffened as she saw the reason. Neil had grabbed something from the ground—a tire iron. He lunged toward Mark, swinging the iron in his hand. Mark twisted, trying to escape the blow, but he was not fast enough. While Laura and Jeannie watched terror stricken, he fell limply to the grass.

Neil did not wait to see how successful he had been. He made a dash for his car. The engine roared to life and the car surged forward, squealing into the street.

He didn't even look in their direction as he roared past the two women.

"Mark!" Jeannie broke free from Laura's arms and ran across the lawn to her fallen husband. Laura followed her.

Mark's eyes were open. He was alive and conscious, although the wound on his forehead was bleeding profusely. Jeannie dabbed at it with the sleeve of her robe. "Better bring him inside," Laura told her gently. "I'll get something to dress the cut."

It was only with the help of the two of them that Mark was able to stand at all, and between them he managed to make it inside the house.

None of the cuts and bruises seemed to be serious. Laura dressed them as best she could, and Jeannie helped.

"Guess I'd better make us some coffee," Laura decided finally. Mark stretched out on the sofa with Jeannie kneeling at his side.

"I'd love some," Jeannie told her with a smile of gratitude.

"Me too," Mark agreed with more enthusiasm than he had been able to display for some time.

Laura left them and went into the kitchen. While she made the coffee, she thought of the suitcase she had packed earlier, still waiting by the front door. She had planned to be gone long before this. What changes all of the subsequent events would necessitate, she did not know. There were Mark and Jeannie to be considered. More than likely, they would want to call the police.

And there was Neil himself. He had been nothing more than a madman when he left. Should his condition be reported? Was it wise to leave him on the loose, not knowing what direction his violent fury would turn next?

She had thought the worst of her problems were behind her. Suddenly that was not true. Things were no better than before, perhaps even worse.

CHAPTER FOURTEEN

Laura stood at the window of her kitchen, staring out at the darkened patio beyond. It was night, several hours after Neil had left, and still no sign of him, nor word.

Jeannie came into the kitchen. "Hey, you aren't supposed to be standing around by yourself. How about some more coffee?"

"Thanks," Laura answered, smiling wanly. She poured herself a fresh cup of coffee and returned with Jeannie to the living room.

"You know, you two don't have to hang around here," she said, glancing from Jeannie to Mark. "I can wait by myself."

"Nothing doing," Mark insisted, shaking his head stubbornly. "We'll all wait here for that ape to get home. I still think we should have called the police."

"No," Jeannie told him anxiously, her eyes widening.

"I can understand that," Laura agreed calmly. "This has been bad enough for Jeannie, without the sort of publicity it would get in the papers. But to tell you the truth, I can't see what any of us can accomplish."

"We've got to try," Mark argued. "If it's nothing

more than talking to him. He needs help, damn it. He can't go around doing that sort of thing."

Laura sipped her coffee morosely. "That's true enough, but you surely don't think it's going to do any good talking to him. You know he was beyond reason, and he certainly isn't going to be any more sober when he gets home."

"Then let's call the police," Mark repeated.

"No, Mark, please," Jeannie pleaded.

"All right, at least not just yet," he agreed. "But if he's in the same sort of shape when he comes home...."

The front doorbell rang sharply. Laura jumped up, spilling her coffee.

"It can't be Neil," she told them, although no one had asked. "He certainly wouldn't ring the doorbell."

Frightened of what she might find, she hurried to the door and flicked on the light outside, looking out through the peephole in the door. To her amazement, she saw two men in dark uniforms.

"The police," she whispered to Mark and Jeannie.

"Mark," Jeannie gave her husband an accusing look. "Did you...?"

He shook his head vigorously. "You know I didn't."

"Well," Laura decided. "There's not much I can do but let them in."

She unlocked the door and opened it timidly, peering outside.

"Mrs. Neil Abbott?" the first of the two officers greeted her.

"Yes," Laura answered, holding her breath. "What

can I do for you?"

"May we come in," the other officer wanted to know.

Laura hesitated for a moment. *Good Heavens,* she scolded herself, opening the door wide, *I haven't broken any laws.*

"Of course," she said aloud.

The officers followed her into the living room. They gave Jeannie and Mark puzzled glances, taking note of the couple's cuts and bruises.

"What seems to be the trouble?" Laura wanted to know, recalling the attention of the officers to herself.

"It's about your husband," one of them explained. "There's been an accident. Seems he had been drinking, and he was driving a little too fast up through the canyon. He missed a curve."

The officer paused, allowing her time to digest the information.

"Neil was hurt?" Laura asked finally.

"Your husband's dead," the officer informed her.

Laura stared blankly at him for a moment. "Dead?" she repeated incredulously.

He nodded. Laura stepped back from him, seating herself slowly on the sofa. Neil was dead! So it was over, the entire nightmare. Jeannie was avenged. No one else would suffer as a result of his frustration and anger.

She wondered whether it had been truly an accident. Neil had hated himself, and his life. There was no hope. He must have known he could never again be more than half a man. He must have feared that Mark and Jeannie would report him to the police. He must have dreaded the public humiliation.

She could envision him, racing madly along the canyon road, all of these things running through his mind, seeing the sign warning of the curve ahead in the road. Time enough to hit the brake and slow down. But if one didn't want to make the curve, or didn't care, how easy it would be to crush the accelerator to the floor, drive into the blackness of the night....

"You all right, Mrs. Abbott?" It was one of the officers speaking to her, calling her back to the present. She smiled faintly, wishing Neil peace. For him, too, the nightmare was ended, and she was genuinely glad he would not have to suffer any more.

"Yes," she told the officers evenly. "Yes, I'm all right now."

CHAPTER FIFTEEN

Laura stood for what she hoped was the last time at the back door of the house at Sandy Knoll and stared across the patio in the direction of the ocean. The real estate agent to whom she had entrusted the sale of the house had assured her that he would have no difficulty in selling the property. It would not be necessary for her to set foot inside the place again.

It was quite sad. She had had such hopes for this house, such childish dreams of happiness. They had prevented her from facing the truth. She should never have married Neil under the awful circumstances which had existed. She would never have fallen into the humiliation of immorality and tragedy that had affected her and Neil, Mark, and Jeannie.

She smiled down at the note in her hand. It was in Jeannie's easy, neat writing. There were no promises, no commitments in it. But Jeannie had given her the address of the apartment building to which she and Mark had moved.

Laura looked up again. Across the way, the same agent who was handling her house came out the back door that had been Jeannie's. He was followed by a young couple.

Laura studied them from the protective shadow of her doorway. How innocent and happy they looked. She had a fleeting urge to run to them, tell them of what might be in store for them. But perhaps, she told herself, they would be happy here. Perhaps they would not have her problems, nor make her mistakes.

She thought of the other couple who had since purchased one of the new houses at Sandy Knoll. She was certain they would get along well with the Blairs. Indeed, Eve Blair had already taken the lovely redhead under her wing.

As if on summons, Eve stepped out into her patio. She, too, looked across the way at her prospective new neighbors, turned and came in Laura's direction. Laura came very near to closing the door and moving away into the interior of the house.

"No, I've done enough running," she decided and remained where she was.

"I guess you'll be leaving soon," Eve greeted her. She did not ask to come inside, nor did Laura invite her in. There had been little association between them since Neil's death.

"The cab's on its way now," Laura informed her. Try as she might, she had found, like Jeannie, that she could not hate Eve. It was not Eve who had caused her unhappiness. The seeds had been there already, within herself and within the marriage. Eve had only followed her nature. She could not be blamed for the fact that Laura had been all too vulnerable to her approach.

"You don't have to leave so soon," Eve reminded her. She seemed strangely more subdued and sincere than was ordinarily the case. "Hank and I would be happy to put you up until things are more settled."

"No, thank you," Laura answered without malice in her voice.

The answer was sufficient. Eve accepted it gracefully. "Maybe we'll see you sometime, anyway," she said with a smile.

"Maybe," Laura answered.

There was nothing more to be said. Eve left, turning to wave once more before she disappeared into her home.

Laura walked into the living room, looking about to see if she had missed anything she wanted to take with her. She was not taking much. The furnishings she was leaving with the house. They held no value for her, only the memory of bitterness and frustration.

She did not hear Hank Blair come into the house. She turned to see him standing in the doorway from the kitchen, watching her. She was reminded of another time he had come into the house to watch her.

"I came to say good-bye." If Eve had seemed subdued, Hank remained the same as always, arrogant and smug. His smile was still sardonic and confident.

"Thought I might give you a going-away present," he went on when she did not answer, coming across the room toward her. "Something to remember me by, as they say in the song."

Laura still said nothing. He took her silence apparently for consent, or perhaps he did not care whether he had her consent or not. In any case, he took her into his-arms without hesitation. She felt the heavy touch of his hands groping their way along her back, over the flaring curve of her buttocks.

The honking of a horn from the driveway interrupted the scene.

"My cab," she told him simply, drawing away from him.

"Send him back," Hank told her, pulling her to him again. "I'll drive you into town later."

He kissed her roughly, demandingly. His hand went boldly to her breast, crushing it beneath the fabric of her blouse.

Laura pulled away from him again, gently but firmly, pleased to discover that she was unaffected by either his kiss or his touch. He held no fascination for her now, no promise of momentary escape from any awful experience.

"Good-bye, Hank," She told him evenly. She did not wait for him to say anything further, nor even watch his reaction, but turned and walked away, picking up her suitcase from the floor.

He was still standing there, looking after her in disbelief when she closed the door and turned the key in the lock. Without another backward glance, she walked quickly down the steps, toward the waiting cab.

ABOUT THE AUTHOR

VICTOR J. BANIS is the critically acclaimed author ("...a master storyteller"—*Publishers Weekly*) of more than 200 published novels and numerous shorter works in a career spanning nearly a half century. A longtime Californian, he lives and writes now in West Virginia's beautiful Blue Ridge region.

www.ingramcontent.com/pod-product-compliance
Lightning Source LLC
Chambersburg PA
CBHW050756250626
47155CB00005B/2091